A DAPHNE AND VELMA MYSTERY

THE VANISHING GIRL

A DAPHNE AND VELMA MYSTERY
THE VANISHING GIRL

BY JOSEPHINE RUBY

SCHOLASTIC INC.

ISBN 978-1-338-59272-6
10 9 8 7 6 5 4 3 2 1 20 21 22 23 24
Printed in the U.S.A. 23
First printing 2020
Book design by Katie Fitch

A DAPHNE AND VELMA MYSTERY
THE VANISHING GIRL

PROLOGUE

In the darkness between dusk and dawn . . .

The girl creeps slowly through the silent night. At this hour, even the shadows are asleep. But she has been summoned. She answered the call, slipped unseen along empty streets, and now approaches a wrought iron gate. She wraps trembling fingers around the cold metal key she's been given. Inserts it in the lock, hoping it won't fit.

It fits perfectly. Turns easily. She pushes, and the gate creaks open. The girl looks to the moon, as if hoping for a sign, an answer, an escape from the trap she's set herself. The moon is silent as the night. So the girl steps inside.

She's old enough to know better. Young enough to ignore the voice in her head saying no, *saying* don't, *saying* turn back before it's too late.

She's a smart girl.

She knows it's already too late.

Beyond the gate lies a land from another time: saloons and stockades, old rail cars and rusted mining carts. Or so it's meant to seem. On these acres of land, nearly three hundred years ago, the town of Crystal Cove was founded. Fifty intrepid settlers docked ship on the edge of what would someday become California. They pitched camp, built homes and churches and schools, made a life for themselves, for one year . . . then disappeared.

Every last one of them.

A century later, the town was reborn, again in this very spot, an outpost for miners desperate for gold, and again, homes were built, fortunes were made and lost, lives were lived, until one night, a spark lit a single building on fire.

By morning, the town was nothing but ash.

The town, some say, is cursed. All those who make the mistake of trying to live there, build there, thrive there are ultimately doomed.

The girl doesn't believe in curses. She doesn't care for history. She doesn't worry about whether there are spirits of the centuries-dead lurking in shadows, watching her. She knows this place only as it is now: a tourist attraction, a ghost town and amusement park trading on its nightmare past. She has been here on school trips; she has napped through dull demonstrations of panning for gold. She has screamed on the Ghost Coaster. She has kissed boys in the Haunted Mine.

Of course, she has never come here alone, at night. Everything looks different in the dark.

A howl echoes in the distance. The girl flinches, and then laughs at her nerves. This is coyote country, she knows that. Their barks haven't scared her since she was a child. Even back then, they didn't scare her much. She was almost fearless, everyone said so. Still, she takes out her phone, types out a text.

this place is SUPER creeptastic

maybe I should get out of here?

It's past two a.m., but the answer comes with furious speed.

why ask me

you already know my answer

"Jerk," she says out loud, and the sound of her voice calms her. She pockets the phone. She is still fearless. She keeps going, past the Spook-O-Wheel and the I Scream for Ice Cream shack, past the cavernous mouth of the Haunted Mine and the one attraction that's always unsettled her, the Mirrored Cave. She hates caves.

She hears a noise behind her, stops cold. It sounded like a footstep. Then another.

"Hello?" She says it very softly. Turns, using her phone as a flashlight. Holding it out before her like a shield.

There's no one there. But when she turns back and starts

walking again, she hears something else. A soft rustling. A scraping. Less like footsteps, more like something being dragged through the dirt. Or someone.

She whirls around again—still nothing. Get it together, *she tells herself.* Get this over with.

Before she can, cold fingers close over her shoulder. A whisper in her ear.

We've been waiting for you.

The girl opens her mouth and lets loose a bloodcurdling scream.

Scream all you want, *the whisper says as an iron grip drags her into darkness.*

There's no one there to hear.

VELMA

"JINKIES!" I WHISPER-SHOUTED INTO the early morning darkness. There was only silence.

"Jinkies!" A little louder this time. Still, silence. Until . . . the soft crack of a twig. Padding footsteps. Then two yellow eyes, blinking out of the dark.

"Come here, you little monster." I scooped up Jinkies, cuddled the fuzzy kitten tight, then deposited her inside with fresh bowls of food and water. The moment she smelled the food, she forgot my existence. Typical cat.

I know it violates every law of teenage life, but I have to admit: I like waking up early, the sky all pink and smeary with dawn, the whole world asleep. No one to see you, no one to judge you, no one to ask you why you are the way you are and not the way they want you to be. No one to look straight through you without bothering to ask anything at all. Just Jinkies and me, up with the sun.

Our apartment was dead quiet. I tried to be quiet, too, though there wasn't much need. My mother worked the overnight shift and wouldn't be home for another couple hours. My father, who could sleep through a jackhammer, usually didn't get up till noon—which, okay, was reasonable on a Sunday. If I tell you he slept that late every day, though, and even once he got up usually stayed in his pj's for another couple hours, staring out the window or listening to depressing music and waiting for the time to pass, you might have some questions.

I had some questions. But I knew better than to ask them. The Dinkley house wasn't exactly a model of open and honest communication. We loved each other. But that didn't mean we knew how to talk to each other. Not about anything real.

When my grandmother was still alive, mornings were our time together. She would wake up even earlier than I did, and the smell of cinnamon toast or, if I was really lucky, chilaquiles, would drag me out of bed and into the kitchen. It was our secret Sunday ritual, just the two of us, talking at the table, about anything and everything—with her, there was no question I wasn't allowed to ask.

But that was a long time ago. Back when we lived in a house with plenty of bedrooms and a big backyard, instead of this tiny apartment where everything was always broken and I slept on a futon shoved into an oversized closet and pretended it was a bedroom. Back when my parents both had jobs they loved and I had a best friend I loved and life was basically okay—back when I was too young to realize things could be any other way.

Jinkies's little hide-and-seek act had almost made me late for work, but I pedaled faster than the rickety old bike had ever managed to go, and showed up right on time (if a little bit sweaty). The Crystal Cove Haunted Village wasn't exactly a village, but then, it wasn't haunted, either, at least as far as I knew. Truth in advertising wasn't really what they were going for.

What they were going for: A tacky, tourist-revenue-generating combination of educational historical exhibits and hair-raising amusement park rides fueled by a steady stream of greasy food, sugary drinks, and all the overpriced crap your kid could beg you to buy. It was another reason to like the early mornings—on days when my shift started before the park opened, I could count on at least a couple hours free from little kids screaming and puking, rude customers expecting me to pretend they were right, and jerky jocks and their plastic girlfriends who ignored me in school but still expected me to slip them free pizza and ride tickets and thought it was hilarious to smear cotton candy in my hair or steal my glasses when I refused.

It's not exactly the part-time job you'd expect I would

have. If you saw me on the street, checked out the turquoise streak in my hair, the chunky glasses, the combat boots, you'd figure me for a record-store geek or some hipster clocking hours in an anarchist bookstore that smelled like incense. Not that there were any anarchist bookstores in Crystal Cove, or any record stores left, anywhere, but you get the picture. Working at the Haunted Village was sometimes dull, sometimes dirty, sometimes humiliating, almost always lame, but it was the best job I could get, and we needed the money. It also felt a little like home. Maybe because it used to be.

Long story.

Anyway, the Haunted Village was filled with fake 1850s-style stores (alongside all the real ones where you could buy your made-in-China souvenirs). It was my glamorous job to unlock them, turn on the lights, and make sure no animals had done any damage—or left any disgusting little treats behind—in the night. The giant gates at the entrance did a pretty good job keeping out any troublemaking humans, but the raccoons and coyotes still somehow found a way inside.

It was usually a pretty uneventful part of the job, and that Sunday started off no differently. The candle-making store was fine, the apothecary fine, the mining outfitter fine . . . and then came the sheriff's department. I stopped short just before opening the door. Something inside was yowling.

It sounded like a wounded cat or a rabid raccoon or, well, I'm not really a nature girl so I had no idea what it sounded like, except like something I was in no hurry to meet.

I could have gone to get the night manager. But the night manager happened to be my mother, and I wasn't especially eager to get my mommy to do my job for me. I could also have gotten the day manager, but Jerry Printz was my mother's boss, and also an annoying twerp always looking for infractions to cite and pay to dock. It had taken me months to convince him I was responsible enough for this shift—I wasn't about to make it seem like I couldn't handle myself with an angry raccoon.

I unlocked the door, opened it, and—

Okay, I admit it.

I screamed.

Just for a second.

And only because the moment I opened the door, I realized that was no angry raccoon. It was a person. Screaming her head off. It startled me enough that I screamed back. Then I took a breath, and a closer look.

"Marcy?" I said. "What are you doing in there?"

It was definitely Marcy Heller, second-prettiest girl in the junior class—though she took first prize when it came to meanest, if you ask me—locked inside the fake jail cell. (Fake cell, real lock—the better to spook little kids with.) She was rattling the bars, shrieking at me to let her out.

I'd known Marcy my whole life—technically, we were second or third cousins, although in a town this small that's not much of an achievement—and I'd almost never seen her with a hair out of place. But that day, her hair was a rat's nest, her eyes were wild, her cheeks mascara streaked, her skin pale as a sheet of paper. She looked like . . . well, she looked like someone who'd spent the night alone trapped in a haunted jail. She looked scared out of her mind.

I fumbled for the keys, opened the doors of her cage. "Are you okay? What are you doing here?"

She didn't say anything.

"What happened, Marcy?" I put a hand on her shoulder, but she shrugged me off, hard.

"Like I'd tell *you*," she snapped. "Take me to see someone in charge."

That sounded a lot more like the Marcy I knew, the one who didn't think I counted.

"Fine," I said, and I made sure there wasn't a shred of concern in my voice. "Let's go."

I brought her to the managers' office, which technically belonged to Jerry Printz, but my mother got to squat in it during her overnight shift. Lucky her. She was still there, handing off the details of the night to Jerry. I introduced Marcy, who was suddenly looking a lot more upset again—the moment we walked into the office, she started crying so hard she couldn't speak. Which left me.

"I found her locked inside the jail," I said. "I think she's been in there most of the night."

Marcy nodded.

"How would that possibly have happened?" Jerry turned to my mother. "You didn't check before you closed down last night?"

"Of course I checked," she said. "She wasn't there when the park closed."

Marcy sniffed and mumbled something that sounded like "after that."

"How would you have gotten in here after hours, young lady?"

This time, Marcy's answer was a lot clearer. "The gate was unlocked."

Jerry's glare swiveled back to my mother; it was the most basic part of her job to make sure all the park gates were locked at night. And she insisted she'd done so.

Which meant someone was mistaken, or someone was lying. Either way, I was absolutely sure that someone wasn't my mother. Jerry Printz, on the other hand, didn't look so sure.

"Velma, why don't you leave us alone so we can get to the bottom of this."

"Why should I leave when—"

"Velma."

When my mother says my name in that tone of voice,

I know better than to argue. I left her there to fend for herself, which I knew was how she wanted it.

But I still felt like a total traitor.

* * *

Once the park opened, my job was to staff the register at the Pizza Panic booth. It was a good shift for a Sunday morning, because no one in their right mind wanted pizza for breakfast. Well, no one, except—

"Can I get, like, six slices, with extra olives, extra jalapeños, extra pineapple, extra anchovies, and, like, extra everything else you got?" That was Shaggy Rogers, for whom every time was pizza time. "And, like, some crusts for Scoob?" Shaggy grinned, and the Great Dane he brought with him everywhere barked hungrily.

"Hey, Scooby," I said, like he was an old friend, which I guess technically he was. I've known Shaggy since we were six years old and Scooby-Doo was just a wriggly little puppy. Dogs weren't allowed in the park, but somehow Shaggy had managed to wrangle himself an exception. My father would have said, *Like father, like son*—just like a Rogers to think the rules didn't apply to him. But I thought it was just that everyone in town loved Scooby-Doo, or at least understood how much Shaggy loved him, and acted accordingly.

And of course, my father didn't have much to say about anything these days.

"Don't you think it's a little early for pizza, Shaggy?"

"Like, it's never too early for pizza."

It wasn't that unusual for Shaggy to wander into the park this early looking for greasy food. He liked to go surfing at sunrise, and the Haunted Village was on his way home. But that day, something about him seemed off.

"You okay, Shaggy?"

He looked like he hadn't slept. Don't get me wrong—Shaggy always looks like he hasn't slept—there's a reason everyone calls him Shaggy. But he was looking particularly ragged. Almost like he was worried about something. Which was weird, because Shaggy's whole life philosophy was to never worry about anything, except where the next snack was coming from.

"It's all good," he said.

That was part two of his life philosophy. Everything was always all good. I'd known Shaggy forever, but never that well. I'm not sure anyone knew him that well. He seemed easygoing, which made sense, because from the outside, he had a ridiculously easy life. He lived in a huge—if slightly spooky—mansion, and his father had a piece of every business in town. His mom was a cop, though rumor had it her husband wanted her to quit her job. Maybe because he was into the whole stay-at-home parenting thing. Or maybe because (again, as my father liked to say, back when my father said things), it's tricky to bend the law when you're married to it. That didn't stop Shaggy from throwing huge parties whenever his parents left town, which they did almost every month. At Crystal Cove High, that was pretty much all you needed to be popular.

Shaggy could have had all the friends he wanted; he probably could have been homecoming king. (If you could get past the scraggly beard and the faded T-shirts two sizes too big, he was almost handsome, though I never would have told him so.) But Shaggy had never had close friends; he'd certainly never had a girlfriend. And he didn't seem to care. He didn't care about much of anything, as far as I could tell, except his stomach and his dog. I liked that about him. He was simple. Sometimes it seemed to me like everyone I knew was wearing a mask, trying to hide who they really were. Shaggy was always just Shaggy.

"You're looking a little rattled yourself, V. *You* doing okay?"

I *was* a little rattled. I couldn't stop thinking about Marcy, how she'd ended up there—and what she was going to do about it. So I told Shaggy the whole story, figuring he'd laugh it off, the way he laughed everything off, and maybe I could steal a little piece of his chill.

Except that when he heard the story, Shaggy's chill vaporized.

"Like, *whoa*. Was she hurt? Did she say what happened?"

"She seemed fine?"

He looked unconvinced.

"I mean, shaken up, yeah. But okay? I—"

"I gotta go," he said, cutting me off. "Come on, Scoob."

"But—"

"Party this weekend, V. You should come." He tossed this over his shoulder as he was walking away, even though we both knew there was no chance in hell I'd ever show my face at one of his parties. But that wasn't the strange part. It was a running joke between me and Shaggy, that one day I would wake up and decide to become one of the party people.

The strange part was that usually he stuck around to actually enjoy the joke, plaguing me with all the "temptations" I was missing out on, promising me how much I would love hearing Luna Moss rock it as a DJ or watching Fred Jones show off his yoga poses, before inevitably toppling, fully clothed, into the pool. I would tell him it wasn't my scene, he would tell me I didn't know until I tried, and I would give him a free slice of pizza to get him to go away.

Everybody's got a thing. That was ours. So it was weird that he ran off so quickly—and even weirder, I suddenly realized as I heard Scooby mournfully barking in the distance, that he'd left without his pizza.

It was a morning full of bad omens. Maybe I should have expected what came next.

But first, a long, dull stretch without any customers. A lot of time to stare at the sky and count how many minutes stood between me and the rest of my life, beyond Crystal Cove and all its history.

Next, my mother, carrying a big cardboard box, looking miserable.

"I just came to say goodbye, and . . ." She trailed off, as if she didn't know what to say. Which was not like my mother at all.

"What's wrong?"

She sighed. "I've been suspended, mi amor. Because that girl claims I left the gate open. There's going to be an investigation of whatever happened in here last night, but given how things are going . . . I'd say it's probably best I start looking for a new line of work."

"They can't fire you!"

She laughed, and inside that laughter was the whole sad story of the last six years. And all the years before that, the happy ones, when all this belonged to us. Or at least, that's what I'd thought.

Before this was a giant, expensive, neon tourist trap with a virtual reality arcade and a waterslide, it was a little museum of local history. No flash, no pizzazz, no plastic souvenirs, only a few dusty display cases and my parents leading tours of schoolchildren through Crystal Cove's cursed past. Only a house next door, big enough for all of us to spread out—though it's funny, because back then, in that big house, everything always felt cozy and together. It's only now, in the tiny apartment we had to move to, that home feels like nothing but empty space.

My mother smiled sourly. "I've learned by now 'they' can do whatever they want." She didn't just sound miserable, she sounded defeated, and Angie Dinkley *never* sounded defeated.

Marcy did this, I thought, furious. She was up to something, and no way was I letting her take my family down in the process.

"Where is she?" I said, fuming.

"Who?"

"Marcy."

"Don't say it like that," she said. "And please don't get involved. Marcy's still in there giving Jerry more details about what happened. Poor girl, she seems totally traumatized. And before you ask, no, I can't give you any more information—it's all confidential and I'm in enough trouble already."

"Because you supposedly forgot to lock up? As if you'd ever do that?"

She shrugged. "Anything is possible. I'm the night manager, Velma. It's right that whatever happens falls on my shoulders."

"Mom—"

She shook her head. Dinkley-speak for *no more talking about this*. I'd just add it to the long list of everything else we never talked about. "I'll see you at home."

Here's what I knew just as well as my mother: She was the most responsible person in Crystal Cove. And on top of that, she loved this place like it was still her own, and would never, ever have forgotten to lock up.

Here's what I knew that my mother didn't, because my mother was a pure-hearted idealist who wanted to see the best in people, and I was a realist who only wanted to see the truth: Marcy was a liar and a troublemaker. And I was going to stop this trouble in its tracks.

I abandoned my post at Pizza Panic and headed to the managers' office to give Marcy, Jerry, or whoever else I could find a piece of my mind. Perfect timing: I found Marcy on her way out, looking a whole lot more like herself. By which I mean smug. And satisfied. She brushed straight past me as if I wasn't even there.

"I need to talk to you!" I hurried after her.

She walked faster, heading for the exit.

"Marcy! Stop acting like I'm invisible!"

Marcy pushed through the front gate. A sleek silver Mercedes was idling at the curb.

"Leave me alone, Dinkley," Marcy said, finally acknowledging my existence. "I've got important places to be. Like my bed." She opened the passenger door of the Mercedes and climbed in.

"Your lies are going to get my mother fired!" I shouted.

Marcy snorted. "If you knew anything about anything, you'd be thanking me. She's getting off easy." Then she slammed the door.

I was about to respond, loudly, using several unmentionable words to colorfully express exactly how unthankful I felt, when the tinted driver's-side window rolled down and a perfectly symmetrical face topped with perfectly wavy, perfectly auburn hair peeked out and fixed me with a perfectly poisonous gaze.

"Your face is turning purple, Velma," Daphne Blake said.

It was the seventh sentence she'd said to me that year. Not that I was counting.

"That can't be healthy," she added, perfectly sweet. Everything about Daphne Blake was perfect, including the perfect sheen of ice in her eyes as she stared right through me. "Ever considered meditation?"

I opened my mouth.

I shut it again.

"Yoga?" she said. Then, worst of all, she laughed. That was stupidly perfect, too. Like a melody.

I hated her. I hated her with the molten heat of the Yellowstone supervolcano, the one so big that when it finally blows it'll cover the entire continent with a layer of burning ash, which will destroy the atmosphere and block out the sun and basically bring about the end of the world.

Actually, maybe I hated her more than that.

A brief interlude, to explain why the sight of a sweetly smiling Daphne Blake was enough to make my tongue curl up in my mouth, my blood turn into pudding, and my heart burst into a fiery ball of rage.

Once upon a time, we were inseparable. Since day one of day care, according to my mom, who has told this same nauseating story approximately one billion times. Some obnoxious toddler pushed Daphne into a mud puddle, and I threw a toy truck at his head and then gave Daphne the rest of my juice box to make her feel better.

That's what they tell me, at least. I have no memory of this, and if I could go back in time, I'd shake that toddler's hand, because he was obviously a lot smarter than I gave him credit for.

They say opposites attract and all, and maybe it's true, because from the outside, Daph and I seemed a lot like opposites. She was the pretty one, I was the smart one—or at least, that's how people treated us. But *I* knew Daph was super smart, and she always told me I was beautiful. The way she said it, I actually believed her.

We were best friends, and we had the BFF necklaces to prove it. We pushed our desks together in school and we had sleepovers every weekend, but the best part of the year was always summer, when we could spend all day, every day, together, finding adventures.

The best summer—which also turned out to be the last summer—was the summer we both turned ten years old, when we decided to be detectives. We lived in a haunted town, right? So why not chase down some ghosts? Not that I ever believed in ghosts—that was Daph's thing. I didn't really care what we investigated, I just wanted a mystery. A whole mystery-solving agency, actually, and so we recruited the boys who lived down the street from her, Fred Jones and Shaggy Rogers. And, of course, Scooby-Doo.

This wasn't unprecedented. The boys never had anything to do on summer vacation, so they usually ended up doing whatever we told them to do. (When we were eight, Daph and I ran a circus—the boys were our clowns. When we were nine, Daph and I were magicians. We made Fred disappear and spent all summer trying to saw Shaggy in half.) We used my parents' van for our office, and I'm proud to say that for that summer we were the most successful detectives in town.

Okay, we were the only detectives in town, and one of us was a dog. And yes, Shaggy was mostly in it for the free snacks and Fred was never into much of anything, but Daph and I were committed. We found some kid's missing pet frog. We helped a third-grader investigate whether there was really a tooth fairy (spoiler alert: There was not). And we spent a lot of afternoons sitting in the van, eating cookies, telling ourselves stories of bigger, better mysteries—monsters lurking in shadowy basements, enchanted suits of armor, ghosts and goblins, all of them taken down by us, Mystery Inc.

Maybe it was a little silly. Kid stuff. Maybe we would have

ditched it in the fall, just like we did with all our other summer games. Maybe we even would have ditched each other, eventually, the way childhood best friends sometimes do—grown apart, naturally, and without the pain that felt like yanking out a tooth. Or sawing off a limb.

But we never got that chance, because that was the summer everything blew up. I don't know how long my parents suspected that the town was going to sell the museum (along with the land, along with our house), but in July some obnoxiously handsome lawyer started poking around on behalf of his anonymous clients. That's when Daph and I finally clued in to what was going on, and we decided it should be our next case. Forget ghosts, we were going to save the museum.

We just didn't quite agree on how to do it. Daph thought the lawyer was the key: It was fishy, right, that he had these secret clients? If we could figure out exactly who wanted to buy the land, then maybe we could stop them. I thought we should focus on finding the original deed to the land, which had been lost a hundred years before. According to my father, his grandfather always claimed that this land once belonged to the Dinkleys. If that was true, and we could find some way to prove it, we could save the day.

But I had no idea where to start looking for a deed, and the lawyer was right there in front of us, so Daph won. We spied on him whenever he came to snoop around the museum. We followed him around town. As far as I could tell, he was the most boring man alive. But then, at that age, all adults seemed breathtakingly boring.

I wanted to give up; Daph insisted on one last stakeout, and I loved her for it, because she wanted to save my parents' business as much as I did.

The only problem was that midway through our stakeout, Daph had to leave for a dentist appointment. So I spent the afternoon following Mr. Handsome and Boring all by myself—to the coffee shop, to the magazine stand, to a secluded corner of the park. He stood under a tree, checking his watch.

My heart beat faster—maybe this was it, what we'd been waiting for, his secret rendezvous with his mystery client.

It was a secret rendezvous, all right.

With Daphne's mother.

Specifically, with Daphne's mother's lips.

You know how they say don't kill the messenger? Well, no one told Daphne. That night, I called Daph and admitted what I'd seen. She didn't want to believe it. She yelled at me, and then hung up on me.

That was the last night we were ever best friends. The next day in school, she told me her parents were getting a divorce, and she said it like it was my fault, and then she wouldn't say anything else to me. She dropped me. Ice-cold. Even when the sale of the museum went through, even when my parents lost their business and our house and my dad basically lost the will to get out of bed, she acted like I was invisible. My mother told me I should be the bigger person, so one day at recess, I tried to talk to her.

Big person, *big* mistake.

To punish me for daring to speak to her like we were still friends, Daphne started calling me Detective Dinkley, and told everyone in school that I was a huge baby who wanted to be a ghost hunter. Marcy, her *new* BFF, started sneaking up behind me and shouting *boo!* all the time, and the other kids thought it was so hilarious that they did it, too. For the whole year. That's when I realized maybe being invisible was the best I should hope for.

In high school, it was easier for Daphne and me to avoid each other. But every time we came face-to-face, I felt like that humiliated ten-year-old girl, the one whose best friend turned on her. The one who learned that maybe it was safest to have no friends at all.

"What?" Daphne said now, all innocent like she couldn't possibly understand why I might be frozen in horror and disgust at the sight of her. "You're staring at me."

That was the worst part of it. Daphne acting like she barely remembered I existed. It was humiliating all over again: Losing her was the worst thing that ever happened to me. But for her, I suspected, it was just little kid stuff. She'd moved on.

"Nothing," I said.

That was how she made me feel. Like a big, invisible, useless nothing.

Daphne smirked, like I'd said exactly what she expected. Then she rolled up the window and drove away.

I went back to Pizza Panic. I served out the rest of my shift. Then I went home, feeling like crap, but putting on a happy face because I figured my mother would need some cheering up. Except my mother wasn't there. According to her note, she was at yet another meeting of her local activist group.

Even now, my mother was a die-hard supporter of Crystal Cove history. She and her friends were trying to make sure the town preserved its character, even as it kept selling off parcels of land to the highest bidder. Right now, every sale came with strings attached. The buyers had to "respect" the town's history and use the land in some way that celebrated Crystal Cove. Which was why the Haunted Village was a Haunted Village and not, say, a golf course. My mom was the queen of the picket sign. If she had her way, the town would stay exactly the way it was, forever. And she wanted to make sure everyone knew it. Which meant I spent a lot of nights alone eating mac and cheese in front of the TV. I made some for my dad, too. He was back in bed.

It was weird, how you could live in the same home as people but still miss them. I missed my mom and dad the way they used to be. I missed our family. Something happened to them when the town took away their museum. It was like that job, that place, anchored them to the ground, and once it was gone, they both just floated away. If it wasn't for Jinkies, mewing for her dinner, it would be easy to believe I really was invisible.

I still didn't believe in things like monsters and curses, but I have to admit: Sometimes I felt like a ghost in my own life.

DAPHNE

I SLAMMED PEDAL TO metal in utter silence, the way Marcy seemed to want it, for as long as I could stand. I was trying, okay? I know that if you go by my history, I wasn't exactly a world-class best friend. People change all the time, right? Why shouldn't one of them be me?

So when Marcy sent an emergency text begging for me to drop everything and come pick her up at the Haunted Village? I dropped everything. I picked her up. When Velma Dinkley tried to spiritually stomp all over her, even though Marcy was clearly in no condition for stomping? I shut her down. And when Marcy put out some serious *don't ask* vibes, I tried not to ask. I seriously did.

Then I broke.

"You going to tell me what's going on, Heller?"

She didn't say anything. Which wasn't natural. Marcy was a talker. We both were. It was one of the many things that bound us together. We both loved talking, but we were reluctant to let most people hear what we had to say. I trusted Marcy enough to tell her anything, and these days I trusted almost no one. She trusted me, too.

I thought she trusted me.

Lately, though, there'd been less talking. Lots more silence. On her end, at first, all these squirrelly non-answers about where she'd been, what she'd been doing, who with. And yeah, maybe I took it personally. Maybe I stopped telling her absolutely everything, too. If only one person in a friendship has secrets, things go out of whack. I figured I should even things out. But it turns out, when two people have secrets? Things go even more out of whack. And it also turns out that it's a lot easier to go out of whack than to force yourself back into it.

"Heller, come on. Spill."

"Don't freak, Blake. It's no big deal."

Marcy was a last name kind of girl. Something else I liked about her. *Blake* sounded like someone cool, someone tough, someone who didn't second-guess every move she made. And with a Heller at my side, I felt like a Blake.

Tough girls don't let their friends carry trouble on their own, I thought.

Tough girls don't let a little broody silence stop them.

"You send me an emergency 911 text at the crack of dawn and show up looking like you spent the night in a sewer," I pointed out. "That's no big deal?"

"Yeah. No. Big. Deal."

Marcy turned away from me. Stared out the window like the streets of Crystal Cove were the most fascinating thing she'd ever seen.

"What's going on with you lately?" I said.

"What do you mean?"

I didn't want to spell it out for her. The classes she was cutting. The fights she kept picking with her boyfriend. The nights she told him she was with me, and told me she was with him, and showed up in the morning as if nothing had happened, and we all just pretended to believe her. Marcy lived on her own, in a little studio apartment that her parents paid for. They were fashion photographers and spent most of their year on the road. Somehow, Marcy had convinced them she was responsible enough to take care of herself. According to Marcy, it had been easy. According to Marcy, they were looking for an excuse to walk away.

There was no one looking over her shoulder, no one who cared enough to ask questions, no one except me. But I couldn't seem to figure out which question would actually get me the right answer.

"Look, can't you just be grateful I gave you an excuse

to get out of there this morning?" she said.

I sighed. Maybe I didn't have any secrets from Marcy after all. She could see right through me. There was nothing I could have wanted more that morning than an excuse to leave the house.

Wait, that's not true. I could have wanted my father to decide he *wasn't* abandoning me for a six-month sabbatical in Tokyo.

I could have wanted my horrible mother and wicked stepfather and bratty half sisters to decide they *weren't* invading my house for six months to keep an eye on me.

I could have wanted to go back in time and stop my parents from splitting up in the first place.

But it was a waste of time to want things you couldn't have. So a temporary escape from watching my father pack and waiting for my mother's limo to show up was probably the best I could hope for.

"Yeah, that's what I thought," Marcy said. Sometimes it felt like she could read my mind.

We were only a couple minutes away from her place. And when I dropped her off, there'd be nowhere to go but back home. I'd have to pretend that I was happy for my dad, who thought getting to go work for some Japanese biologist on some biomolecular I-stopped-listening-before-I-got-the-details was the opportunity of a lifetime.

Then I'd have to watch him pretend to be nice to my

mother and my mother's husband, aka the reason my father was no longer my mother's husband. And we'd all pretend to be delighted by the step-brats, who were technically half-sister-brats, but I didn't want to claim any piece of the wonder twins. Daisy and Dawn, the most perfect five-year-olds who have ever existed. At least according to my mother. Bad enough I had to imagine her replacing us with some picture-perfect insta-family all these years. At least most of the time, she was hours away in San Francisco, and I didn't have to see it for myself. In a few hours, there'd be nowhere else to look.

"Maybe we should just keep driving," I said. "Get out of town, start fresh somewhere else."

Marcy finally turned away from the window and looked at me.

"You mean that?" There was something weird in her voice, almost like a tremble. But Marcy never trembled. She was steel.

I did mean it. Sort of. I mean, I wanted to mean it. I wanted to do it, get away. Eventually. After high school. After college. The way things were done. Maybe *Blake* was the kind of girl who'd just take off into the unknown. But *Daphne* always did things the way things were done. And you couldn't separate one from the other. At least, I couldn't.

"No," Marcy said, and if I hadn't known better, I would

have thought she was trying not to cry. "You don't mean it. So just take me home. Please."

* * *

"You're absolutely, positively sure you want to do this?"

My father zipped up the last of his suitcases.

"Absolutely?" I said.

"Positively," he said.

"You know the flight is about a thousand hours long," I pointed out. "And you hate using airport bathrooms. And you hate jet lag. And, by the way, you hate Japanese food. You don't think that's going to be a problem in Japan?"

"Honey—"

"You're going to miss me so much you won't be able to take it," I told him.

"I'm going to miss you so much I won't be able to take it," he agreed, and he gave me a hug, and I wished I could hang on forever.

"Is now a good time to take advantage of your guilt and get you to let me stay here by myself?" I said.

He laughed. "There is no such thing as a good time for that discussion. As we've already discussed. Many, many times."

"I just don't see why I can't live on my own. Marcy does it."

"Marcy is *exactly* why you can't live on your own."

Okay, so Marcy wasn't exactly my father's favorite person. I'm not sure any adult in town would have said Marcy was their favorite person. Or that she'd even crack the top ten. That was part of her appeal.

"Besides, your mother is eager for the chance to spend some real quality time with you."

"Way to bring down the mood, Dad." I flung myself down on the bed, sighed dramatically, pretended I was pretending to be this upset. Easier than letting him know how I really felt. If he knew how much I was dreading it—him leaving, her staying—he might have canceled his trip after all. And I couldn't do that to him. I may be spoiled—most people seem to think so—but I'm not selfish. I knew I had to let him go.

"She's so excited for this, Daphne. You have no idea how much she misses you."

I could never understand why he was so desperate to lie for her. Even after everything she'd done to him. Too bad his daughter's so good at eavesdropping. I heard him on the phone with her when he first got the news about the Tokyo thing. So I knew exactly how eager my mother was to leave her high-powered life in the big city and spend six months in a small town playing nursemaid to her sullen teenage daughter. She wanted me to come stay with them in San Francisco. Or for all I know, she wanted me to vaporize, so she could forget that the Blake family and Crystal Cove and everything about her life before six years ago ever existed.

I have no idea how my father talked her into taking a sabbatical of her own, running her company out of our house while he was gone. But by the time anyone officially told me about it, everyone was all smiles and *Oh boy, won't this be fun.*

I smiled, too. I was a pro at keeping myself to myself. And lucky for me. Because everyone was always telling me what a beautiful girl I was, and they always said it like they thought being beautiful was the most important thing in the world. If they knew who I really was, deep down? If they knew all the feelings I kept locked up inside, the ugly monster underneath? They'd know there was nothing beautiful about me.

I watched from my bedroom window as my mother's limo pulled up in front of the house. Have I mentioned that my mother is a major media mogul? She didn't exactly fit in to Crystal Cove, even when she lived here. Which is funny, because her entire empire's founded on our town. She designed this video game, *The Curse of Crystal Cove*, back when she was still in college. Fast-forward a few years and pretty much every kid on the planet was playing it.

The real-world town of Crystal Cove is bordered by a sparkling blue sea on one side and snowcapped mountains on the other; we've got towering redwoods and a pristine desert not too far away, and we're an easy drive from San Francisco. There are a ton of reasons for people to want to move here, and for developers to buy up our land. But the number one reason is *The Curse of Crystal Cove*, which means the number one reason is my mom.

I watched her get out of the limo. She just stood there for

a moment, and I wondered if she was nervous. It was so strange to see her back here for the first time since she'd moved out. I could almost fool myself into thinking we were back in time, that she was still the mom I used to know, the one who was there when I woke up in the morning and still there when I went to bed at night. That this was her home again, and I was her family. Then she knocked on the door, and the fantasy fell away. You don't knock on the door of your own home. And if you're a guest, you can't be family.

I heard the door swing open, then, "Daphne, your mother's here!"

I put on my best dutiful daughter smile and tromped downstairs. My mother opened her arms wide. I let them hang there, empty, until she gave up on me and put them down again.

"I'm so happy to be here," she said.

"That makes one of us," I said. But at least I tried to say it quiet enough that no one would hear.

My stepfather came in, carrying the suitcases, and the wonder twins pranced in behind him. They shook everyone's hands. They practically curtsied.

"Daddy, can we go upstairs and read?" one of them said. I had no idea which one. They were identical little blond cherubs, and I figured there was no need to learn which was which. Either way, it wasn't natural, little kids being so well behaved.

My mother directed them up to the guest bedroom,

told them to make themselves at home. It was enraging, watching her act like she still lived here. Like she had any say over anything that happened here.

"They must have thrown a fit when you told them about this trip," I said hopefully.

"They loved the idea," my stepfather said. He looked just like them, blond and boring. "They think it's an adventure."

Like I said. No little kids should be that well behaved.

"I'll wait for your taxi on the porch," I told my father, and walked out without saying another word. Someone was going to have to be the rude, rebellious daughter, and it seemed I was the only remaining option.

As I closed the door behind me, I heard my stepfather telling my mother not to worry, that she'd have plenty of time to soften me up.

I made a promise to myself: I would not let that happen.

It seemed like no time at all before the taxi showed up to take my father away. I gave him one more hug and tried to make it last forever. It didn't work. He held me at arm's length, stared hard.

"What?" I said.

"I'm just trying to memorize your face," he said.

"You'll see plenty of my face. We're Skyping daily, remember?"

He grinned. "I remember. Just testing to make sure you do." He hesitated for a moment. "Do me a favor, Daphne?"

"What?"

"Go easy on your mother."

"It's a big house," I told him. "We can avoid each other."

"I don't want that for you. I want you to know your mom. She's an amazing woman—"

"You don't have to say that."

"You're right. I don't have to say that. So you should know it's true. You deserve to have her in your life."

"Maybe I don't want her in my life."

He sighed. "I guess if I keep trying to argue you into this, I'm going to miss my plane."

"Maybe that's my nefarious plan," I joked.

Sort of joked. Sort of desperately wished he would stay. I ordered myself not to cry. I was sixteen. That was too old to cry over something like this. I told myself to be more like Marcy. Steel.

"I love you, Daphne. Remember that. Try to stay out of trouble."

"It's Crystal Cove," I reminded him. "Most boring place on earth. What trouble could there possibly be?"

* * *

Some very good, very reasonable reasons to hate my mother:

1. She was obnoxiously excellent at everything she tried (except "not cheating on her husband," I guess, and "not destroying her

family"—she was terrible at that). She was a computer genius, who built a huge empire from scratch and gave a ton of her earnings away to programs to help girls get into computer coding and a bunch of other charities, which I knew because every time she did, a million people emailed me to tell me how great she was.

2. In every single science and math and computer class I'd ever taken, the teacher started out assuming I would be a genius, too, because I was Elizabeth Blake's daughter. Then they discovered the truth. And it was like I'd personally betrayed them. Did anyone care that I got good grades in English? No, they did not. I wrote in my journal every night—it was the only safe place to put all my truest, ugliest emotions—but did anyone guess that I might be a writer, or that I could be good at anything except looking pretty? No. They did not.

3. My mother married George Baker, my stepfather. Even after he helped ruin

Velma's life. Velma Dinkley and I might officially be worst enemies, but I still haven't forgiven him for that.

4. Did I mention the whole cheating on her husband, destroying her family thing? Because also: that.

5. The first few weeks after she moved out, I would cry myself to sleep every night. Or at least, I would try to cry myself asleep, but I would just lie awake. I missed her too much. I missed Velma too much. I missed everything about the way my life used to be. And every night, my father would come sit by my bed, and I would pretend to sleep, because I didn't want to worry him. He was never fooled. He would say, "It's okay, Daphne. You can be sad. I'm sad, too." That was the biggest reason I hated my mother. She had made my father so, so sad.

All of which is to explain why I made it about ten minutes into our first "family dinner"—apparently something I would be required to do every night, vomit—before picking a fight.

It wasn't all my fault. My mother asked how school was going. I told her I didn't want to talk about it. She asked how my friends were doing, whether I still hung out with "that nice girl, Velma Dinkley." I told her I *really* didn't want to talk about it. Then my mother suggested we all go out to dinner on Friday night—except "suggest" was more like "insist." She'd already made a reservation.

"I can't," I said. "I'm going to a party."

"Why is there no question mark at the end of that sentence?"

"Because it's not a question," I said. "I'm going to a party."

"Would you like to ask my permission?" she said.

"Dad never makes me ask permission."

"Dad's in Tokyo," she pointed out.

One of the twins piped up. "Actually, if his flight left at four p.m., then he's approximately six hundred miles past—"

"Shut up," I told her.

Yes, I told an adorable, blond, gap-toothed five-year-old to shut up. And when George told me not to talk to my sister that way, I said she wasn't my sister, and then the adorable five-year-old burst into tears.

I know, I'm a monster.

That's when my mother, a few years too late, decided to start mothering me. "Daphne, if you can't sit at the table and have a civilized conversation, go to your room."

"Thought you'd never ask."

I ran upstairs. I slammed my door shut. I burst into tears. Add that to my list of talents: melodramatic teenager. I figured if I was going to spend the next six months of my life completely miserable, the least I could do was make sure their lives were miserable, too.

Part of me figured that.

The other part of me didn't want to be that kind of person, the one who made little kids cry. I told myself I would find a way to be better. Somehow.

I texted Marcy, hoping to get a little moral support, and maybe a little more detail about whatever she'd refused to tell me that morning, but there was no answer. She hadn't texted back all day.

It was starting to feel like everyone who mattered to me had left me behind.

I got my journal from its hiding place in my closet—then set it down without writing anything. It was suddenly too depressing, the idea of listing everything going wrong. I kept the journal in a shoebox, along with all my most important secrets. Including an old notebook, its cover faded, its pages tattered. I almost never let myself look through it, but now I did, turning one page after the other, giving myself permission to remember.

This was the notebook Velma and I kept the summer we played detective, the summer everything fell apart. It was our case log, and our brainstorming book, the place we wrote down every theory we came up with, every clue we found, every adventure we imagined. All of them in Velma's neat handwriting. Even all those years later, I knew it as well as my own.

There was a picture of us tucked into the middle of the notebook. Velma was holding her glasses behind her back, because she hated to be photographed in them. I had my arm around her shoulder, my head pressed against hers. I looked so happy. We looked so happy together.

We thought we would always be best friends. And maybe we would have, if I hadn't ruined things. That was the summer I discovered I had a monster inside me. That I was a person capable of doing terrible, ugly things.

I knew Velma was just trying to help when she told me what she saw. I shouldn't have yelled at her for it—I knew that even as I was yelling. When I told my mother what Velma saw, and my mother said yes, it was true, she was in love with someone else, she and my father were getting divorced, I shouldn't have blamed Velma. That made no sense. I know that now. I knew that then. But I blamed her anyway, and I froze her out, and then, most evil of all, I humiliated her in front of everyone we knew. I guess I thought hurting her would make me hurt less. It very much did not.

Every day after that, I wanted to apologize. But I didn't know how. I didn't have the nerve. I hated myself for that.

Every time I saw Velma's face, I remembered what I'd done, and how much I hated myself for it, and maybe that's how I started hating her a little bit, too.

I texted Marcy again. Still no response. So I went online to see if I could get her to chat, but she wasn't there, either. Which these days wasn't that weird.

What *was* weird? Everyone else we knew was online, and the moment I went green, they all started pinging me, asking me if I'd seen the article, and what I thought was going on with Marcy, and what I knew.

I knew nothing.

Nothing except apparently my best friend was headline news and I was the last to know.

I clicked on the article they were all passing around. The link went to an exclusive interview in our local tabloid. The *Crystal Cove Howler* mostly reported local news—a lot of it fake and the rest of it nasty local gossip—but thanks to my mother making Crystal Cove a household name, the *Howler*'s headlines always made big news. This one read: *Local Teen Terrorized: Crystal Cove Curse Strikes Again?*

I opened the article and read it in disbelief. No wonder everyone wanted the inside scoop I couldn't give them. No wonder Marcy didn't want to tell me the story to my face. Because the story was unbelievable. Literally.

Except that, judging from the comments, half the internet seemed to believe it.

The story: Local teen Marcy Heller was found screaming and terrorized inside a jail cell in the Crystal Cove Haunted Village. She claimed that she'd been ambushed, thrown into the cell, and locked up for the night.

And who would do that to an innocent young girl? "This is going to sound nuts," Marcy told the reporter, "but you have to believe me. It wasn't a who. It was a what. It was a ghost!"

There was something going on in Marcy's life, something big, that was obvious. I couldn't imagine what would make her run to a reporter with such a wild story, or what the reporter had said to drag it out of her. What I knew was that she needed me, but instead of turning to me in her time of need, she turned to a stranger. I wondered if I even still *had* a best friend, if she hadn't somehow decided I was untrustworthy, that I was someone destined to betray her. And if she had, could I blame her?

I'd promised myself a long time ago that I would make up for what I'd done to Velma, that this time around, with Marcy, I would be the best friend anyone had ever had. But I wasn't sure I trusted myself to pull it off. I worried that deep down, I was just a disloyal person, someone destined to hurt the people she loved most.

Maybe that was the real reason I hated my mother. Because a part of me was afraid we were exactly the same.

VELMA

IT'S BEEN SAID—USUALLY behind my back but also plenty to my face—that I can be a bit of a know-it-all. This is not accurate. I know a lot of things, but included among them is the knowledge of how very much I don't know. How much? Well, don't spread this around, but . . . a *lot*. The problem is that when I *do* know something, I have a hard time not saying so. Especially when someone else has just said something that I know to be wrong. You'd think people would find that *helpful*.

Apparently not.

For example: I didn't know everything about Marcy Heller. I didn't know why she'd stayed in Crystal Cove when her parents moved away last year, or why any parents would let their fifteen-year-old daughter get emancipated and live on her own. I didn't know why she cut school so much or did any of the other unwholesome, occasionally illegal things that earned her the reputation of a girl who would do pretty much anything. (Anything she wasn't supposed to, at least.) But here's one thing I did know: Marcy Heller did not get attacked by a ghost.

It was a ridiculous story. Almost as ridiculous as the fact that every time she told it—and she was telling it all over town—more people believed her. Or, at least, they *wanted* to believe her. That was pretty obvious. And in my opinion, that was even worse.

"She did *not* see a ghost," I told Aimee Drake in homeroom, after she spent ten straight minutes telling Sammie Daniels and Aparna Din what her slightly older and substantially cooler sister had heard from Marcy herself.

"There's no such thing as ghosts," I informed my chem lab partners, a trio of big-brained mathletes who should have known better.

"She's lying," I told Mr. Gersick, the janitor, who occasionally came by to talk to me during lunch—most days I ate in the library, but sometimes the sun was so beautiful I couldn't resist lunch on the quad. There was a little grove of trees on the western edge, farther than most people bothered to go, where I could pretend there wasn't a quad full of people laughing and gossiping and doing whatever it was high school students did with their friends.

I don't say that to get sympathy. I could, hypothetically, have had friends, if I'd wanted them. And I suppose it's possible I could have been a little less of a know-it-all, a little friendlier . . . and, okay, maybe a little happier. I could have worn boots that weren't so obviously made for stomping someone's face in. Here's the almost-impossible-to-believe reason for not bothering to sand down all those sharp edges: I wasn't interested in friends. I'd tried that with Daphne, and where had it gotten me? Betrayal, public humiliation, loneliness. What was the point of friends if you were eventually going to end up alone? After Daphne, I figured it was easier to skip the unpleasant middle part and get used to the inevitable. By junior year, I'd gotten *very* used to it. I had my fellow internet gamers, and friends on some of the forums. I had my books, and I had my dreams of a future somewhere very far away from Crystal Cove, in a place filled with people who understood me, wherever that might be. Still, it was nice when Mr. Gersick took a break from emptying the dumpsters to stop and chat.

"How do you know she's lying?" he asked.

"A, because she's a liar," I said. "B, because there's no such thing as ghosts, obviously, even if it's practically against the law in this town to say so."

"Say you're right," he said, grinning. Mr. Gersick loved an argument.

"I'm right," I said, grinning back. I loved one, too.

Our school didn't have a debate team, because no teacher wanted to sponsor it—I'd suggested, the year before, that Mr. Gersick would be perfect for the job, but according to Principal Shenker, a janitor didn't count as a sponsor. Judging from the way most people treated Mr. Gersick, you'd think a janitor didn't even count as a human. That was another reason I hadn't bothered to make friends at Crystal Cove High.

Most people sucked.

"Okay then," he said. "*Why* is she lying?"

That was the biggest thing—the most important thing—I didn't know. Why would Marcy tell this particular lie? Not to mention the lie that was about to get my mother fired, a lie that I had been strictly ordered to leave alone. This was an order I would obviously not be following, even though it came straight from my mother.

"I have no idea," I told Mr. Gersick. "But I swear to you, I'm going to find out."

He shrugged. "The things you kids get yourselves into," he said, chuckling, and headed back to his work.

The things we kids got ourselves into: I knew what that meant, for most kids, even if I mostly knew it from watching TV or overhearing gossip or enduring assemblies from the principal about all the things we were not to do. But pretty much all I ever got myself into was a book. If Marcy wasn't trying to get my mother fired, if my family didn't need that income so desperately, if this whole situation wasn't driving both my parents nuts—my father spending even more time in bed, my mother pouring all her new spare energy into her activist groups, most of them meeting in our kitchen—I would have happily let the whole school believe in ghosts. I wasn't ten years old anymore. I no longer thought it was my job to prove to anyone that our town wasn't haunted. But Marcy's "ghost" was definitely connected to Marcy's lie about how she got into the Haunted Village, and getting to the bottom of that was my job. Because no one else was going to do it.

The only problem was that Marcy was nowhere to be found. Every day, I showed up at school, steeling myself to confront her. And every day she was out, supposedly sick.

Finally, I decided to explore my next-best option: Daphne. I dreaded talking to her—it was sure to lead to yet another humiliation for yours truly—but when I found myself alone with her in the girls' room, I just couldn't pass up the opportunity. So I cornered her.

"Your BFF got herself a pretty convenient flu," I said as I finished washing my hands. She was retouching her makeup, batting her eyelashes at her reflection. Typical. "Or is it 'ghost pox'?"

Daphne didn't answer. She didn't even look at me. I felt my temperature rising.

"This isn't a joke, Daphne. This stupid story she's telling? My mom could lose her job."

Daphne froze, mid–mascara reapplication, and for a second, I thought I actually had her attention. Maybe some tiny part of her remembered how much time she'd spent in my house, eating my mother's cooking, letting my mother help her with her homework or give her advice or, every once in a while, dry her tears. Or maybe she just didn't like hearing me call Marcy's story stupid.

"If you know something that could help . . . anything . . ."

Daphne closed the mascara, slipped it into her bag, and walked straight out of the bathroom. She didn't even look at me. Not once. It was as if I wasn't even there.

I am not a ghost, I reminded myself. *I am not invisible.* No matter how good Daphne Blake was at making me feel that way.

* * *

There is nothing better than the sound of the bell ringing at the end of the school day on a Friday afternoon. Especially that week, which had lasted approximately seven hundred years. Marcy never came back to school. I heard whispers she was dropping out, or getting kicked out—all I knew was that I'd gotten no closer to getting some answers, while my mother was inching ever closer to getting fired.

No one would talk to me about the negligence investigation, but I knew how things worked at the Haunted Village, and in Crystal Cove. Marcy's parents were rich. Important. Even though they no longer lived here, they pumped plenty of money into the town to make sure their precious little girl was well taken care of. The Dinkleys, on the other hand, were nobody. There wasn't going to be an investigation, not really. Jerry would let a few days, maybe even a few weeks, pass, then he would send my mother packing.

I didn't know where that would leave us. I didn't want to know. I just wanted to stop worrying about it, for at least a few blissful hours. That's what Friday afternoon meant to me. Not the start of the weekend—which, for me, was just forty-eight hours of homework and Haunted Village shifts. Friday afternoon, the moment the bell rang, I got to hop on my bike and pedal straight to the library.

I know, I know. If it's not natural for a teenager to like early mornings, it's significantly less natural for her to get that excited about the *library.* And the Crystal Cove Library itself wasn't anything special, I guess, although I would argue every library is something special. I'd loved it since I was a little kid. We could never afford new books (especially at the pace I read, my mother pointed out). But the library would give you as many books as you wanted, as often as you wanted, for free. All you had to do was give them back when you were done. That would have been reason enough to love the library. That and the fact that the girls I hated—girls like Daphne Blake, I mean—would never be caught dead there. But for the last year, I'd found an even better reason.

I locked my bike to the front stairs and went inside. The librarian was running storytime for a bunch of little kids and made them all wave hello to me as I crossed to the very back and through a door marked DO NOT ENTER. The door led to a narrow, tiled hallway with flickering fluorescent light. *That* led to another door, this one locked. I had the key. The door creaked open, and I squinted into the darkness. "Hello?" I whispered. There were no rules about soft voices back in this part of the library, but it was a hard habit to shake.

"I've been waiting for you!" The voice boomed, echoing against the tile floor. Dr. Thomas Hunter had shaken the habit of quiet a long time ago—but then, maybe when you've spent the last thirty years of your life in a library, you get used to treating it like home. "Hurry in, Ms. Dinkley, I've been eagerly awaiting you."

I loved how he called me Ms. Dinkley, as if I was someone important.

"Finally, we can get down to business."

I loved how he treated me like I was essential.

"I have your favorite. Still hot." He handed me a steaming mug of hot chocolate, its edges dusted with cinnamon. "Even though you're approximately two minutes late."

I loved most of all how he actually wanted me there. Sometimes it felt like in this whole town, Dr. Hunter was the only one who'd notice if I disappeared. My parents loved me, of course. I knew that. But they were so wrapped up in their own stuff—my mother with her work and her activist groups, my father with his gloom. Even Jinkies would probably forget me in about thirty seconds if she found someone else to feed her dinner.

Dr. Hunter was a nationally renowned historian who specialized in Crystal Cove's history—specifically, the mysterious disappearance of its original settlers. He belonged in some big, exciting city, at some big, exciting university, but instead he'd chosen to live here and work out of this back room of the library, where he'd spent a decade building his archive. He certainly didn't need me to help him organize it—especially since I usually spent less time organizing than I did oohing and aahing over his latest archival finds—but he acted like he needed me. He acted like it actually mattered that I was there.

I sipped the hot chocolate as Dr. Hunter showed me what he'd found since our last Friday afternoon—it was a map of Crystal Cove from the nineteenth century, brown and curled at the edges, marking out property lines.

"Looks like some kind of tax inspector record?" I guessed.

"Very good. You've been paying attention."

I could feel the warmth in my cheeks, and hoped they weren't too red. I know what you're thinking, but let me be clear: This was not some kind of absurd crush situation. For one thing, Dr. Hunter was *old*. Like, dad-aged old. He had bushy eyebrows, like wriggling caterpillars, and one of his front teeth was yellow. He wasn't even embarrassed about it, or I assumed he wasn't, because he smiled almost nonstop. I'd never met anyone who was so easily delighted. He could play stern—I saw it when our class took a field trip to the archives. Marcy started fiddling with a diary dating back to the gold rush, and he told her, very coldly, that the diary was a lot more valuable than she was and perhaps she should keep her hands to herself. If I was ever going to get a crush, it would have been then. Dr. Hunter wasn't really crush material. He was more like the perfect father and grandfather all rolled into one. He felt sort of like home—but he also felt like its opposite, the promise of a bigger world very far away from here.

"It's not what you're looking for, I'm afraid," he said. "But it does feel like we're closing in."

That was the reason I'd started volunteering for Dr. Hunter in the first place, of course, though it took me a long time to admit it. I was still looking for that mythical deed, the one that would prove my father's family owned the Haunted Village land. Dr. Hunter didn't laugh when I finally told him about it. He said, "*Fascinating.*" And then he promised me that if it existed, we would find it. One Friday afternoon at a time.

After we'd finished marveling at his map, Dr. Hunter set me up with a thick, dusty folder of black-and-white photographs—glimpses of the town from a hundred years ago. I spent the next hour making a list of photo dates and descriptions, sipping hot chocolate, and complaining about how our ghost-loving town had gone even more bonkers for ghosts.

"People will believe anything that confirms their secret fears," Dr. Hunter said. "Once you figure that out, the world becomes somewhat simpler to navigate."

"I don't really care what lies people believe, or why," I told him. "I care about the lies, and who they hurt. If I could just get a chance to ask—"

I stopped short at the sound of a knock on the door.

No one ever knocked on that door.

Dr. Hunter frowned, and then, as if his mental clouds had suddenly parted, his forehead smoothed. "I forgot to tell you, the hot chocolate isn't the only surprise I've got for you today."

"Oh?" I hate surprises.

"We found someone to help you out around here," he said.

"I, uh, didn't realize I needed help."

"Everyone can use some help," he said, approaching the door. The knocking was getting louder. Impatient. "And maybe you know her." He opened the door.

And yes, I knew that glossy scowl. That entitled wrinkle in the nose. The irritated hands on the hips. The cascading waves of red hair. "Daphne?"

"Velma?"

Apparently we still had one thing in common, because when we spoke again, our overlapping voices dripped with precisely the same amount of disgust.

"What are *you* doing here?"

DAPHNE

***WHAT AM I* DOING** *here?* That's all I could think, frozen in that stupid library doorway. That's all any normal human being would think, trapped in all that darkness and dust when there was a perfectly good Friday afternoon just outside.

I should have known I'd find Velma Dinkley, of all people, lurking in there. *Voluntarily.*

Not just because Velma was exactly the kind of person who volunteered to spend her free time with some random old nerd, doing paperwork in a mildewed storage room. But because it was clear that the universe was out to get me.

And it was doing a pretty good job.

Rewind to Monday morning. Maybe the first morning in my life I'd ever woken up before the alarm and flung myself out the door toward school. Eight guaranteed hours away from the house, which no longer felt like mine. Not now that it had been colonized by my mother and the family she liked better than the one she'd started out with.

Bonus: School meant Marcy. An explanation about what was going on. Confirmation that we were still friends, that I was just being insanely paranoid about all the unreturned texts. That everything was the way it had always been and the way it should be.

Except Marcy didn't show up, and then she didn't show up again the next day.

Where are you? I'd texted her on Monday.

Sick, she wrote back.

I'm coming over, I texted. Getting to live alone in your own apartment at age sixteen was, under most circumstances, wildly cool. Under circumstances of flu, however, it was miserable. No one to bring her orange juice. No one to give her fresh sheets. No one to care. Except for me. I always came by when she was sick. I brought along soup, cough drops, cheesy magazines—evidence someone was paying attention.

Contagious, she wrote. **Stay away.**

So she wasn't really sick. I knew that much, at least.

Marcy would never pass up a little TLC just for the sake of sparing me germs.

When she didn't show up at school on Wednesday,

I decided I'd show up instead. I went straight to her doorstep after school. I tried to bring her boyfriend with me, thinking he'd be just as worried. But worry was a human emotion. I'd forgotten that Trey Moloney didn't have many of those.

"Dude, I'm not her boyfriend anymore," he told me. Trey didn't go to class much more than Marcy did. I'd found him in the parking lot, polishing his truck. I was pretty sure he treated that truck better than he'd ever treated Marcy. "You two are basically psychic for each other. You must know that already."

There was almost no way Marcy would have dumped Trey without telling me.

But there was even less of a way I wanted to admit to Trey that he knew something I didn't.

"Pretend I don't."

"Dude, she dumped me right after she saw the 'ghost.' Maybe the ghost made her do it." He waggled his fingers in my face. "Boo!"

"So she dumped you out of the blue, and then called a tabloid and claimed that she'd had a supernatural experience," I said. "And now she's cut school for three days in a row. That doesn't seem kind of extreme, even for Marcy? You're not worried?"

Trey looked kind of like a Ken doll, and he had the brains to match. But surely even he could put those pieces together.

"Something's got to be wrong," I told him.

"The chick was cheating on me. That's wrong. But now she's not my problem anymore. That's right." He edged past me to polish an imaginary spot on his precious truck.

Which is how I ended up on Marcy's doorstep, outside Marcy's empty apartment, all by myself. Waiting.

Call it a stakeout.

An hour passed: no Marcy. Two hours, then three. I was supposed to be home by then. My mother had invited her college best friend for dinner—my godmother, who I liked more than my actual mother. She had made it clear I was supposed to show. Preferably on time and in a polite mood. Which was all the more reason to stay on that doorstep.

Not that I had anything against "Aunt" Emma—she was always nice to me. That didn't mean I was going to just do as I was told, like a good daughter. I *was* a good daughter—but only to my good parent. Which, in case it hasn't been made painfully clear, is not my mother.

Marcy clomped up the stairs just before sunset.

"You don't look sick," I said.

"What are you doing here?"

"What do you think I'm doing here, Heller? I'm your best friend." I tried not to put a question mark at the end of the sentence, but she must have heard it anyway. She sighed and grabbed my hands, pulling me to my feet. Then she unlocked the door.

"Okay, Blake. You might as well come in."

The apartment was a studio, and—since Marcy subsisted on yogurt, granola, and cold pizza—she basically used the kitchen as a giant walk-in closet and had made the rest of the apartment one big bedroom. Marcy dropped with a thump onto her patchwork comforter. I sank back into her beanbag chair. We'd sat exactly like this hundreds and hundreds of times, but this time felt different. Maybe because it was so clear she didn't want me there.

We stared each other down. *She's your best friend*, I told myself. *That doesn't change just because she's mad or upset or keeping some terrible secret or thinks she saw a ghost or whatever's going on. That doesn't change just because she pretends you mean nothing to her. It's a front*, I told myself. *A way to cover weakness.* Marcy didn't do *weak*. Ever.

Except that this time, after a minute or two of silent glaring that felt like it lasted about a hundred years, she broke first. "Okay. What."

Marcy *never* broke first. In Marcy-speak, that was a cry for help.

"Start anywhere," I said. "Where have you been all week? Where were you just now? I won't ask why you dumped Trey"—that was the one thing she'd done that actually made sense—"but why didn't you tell me first? Or, speaking of telling people things, why are you telling people you saw a ghost?"

"You don't believe me?"

"Come on, you're not serious."

"How do you know?"

"Heller, are you not the person who once said the only thing dumber than voluntarily living in this town is coming here on vacation, just because it's supposedly haunted?"

"Sounds like me," Marcy said. "And now that I know how scary real ghosts are, I believe it even more."

Time for a different angle. "What were you even doing there, in the middle of the night?"

She shrugged. "I was walking by, the gate was open. It was there—do I need a better reason?"

"You know they're saying Velma Dinkley's mother might get fired because of you."

She narrowed her eyes. "If anyone gets fired, it'll be because of her negligence. Not 'because' of me. But I'm glad to hear you're more concerned about your ex-best friend than your current one."

It was mean, which was reassuring; mean was Marcy. Especially on the subject of Velma Dinkley. We never talked about it, but we both knew that if I'd stayed friends with Velma, I never would have ended up friends with Marcy. Deep down, I suspected she was jealous.

Even deeper down, I hoped so. Don't forget, I'm a monster.

Marcy stood up. "If that's all you came for—"

"It's not just the so-called ghost; it's not even just this

week. You've been acting . . . different. For a while. I need to know what's going on with you. I can help."

"Huh."

"What?"

"It's just interesting phrasing," Marcy said. "You *need* to know."

"Yeah," I said. "So?" Turns out mean is a little less comforting when it's aimed in your direction.

"You *need* a lot of things, Blake. A person might even call you *needy*. Which is kind of funny, when you think about how much you already have."

"What's that supposed to mean?"

Never ask a question you don't want to know the answer to.

"It means how much whining have you done about your mother uprooting her entire life to come stay with you? How many times have you said you wish she was more like mine? You know, not giving a crap."

Everyone in school thought it was amazing that Marcy's parents had let her live on their own when they took off on their cross-country adventure. Most of the time, Marcy acted like she thought it was amazing, too. But I was the one who was supposed to know better.

"I'm sorry, I—it just didn't occur to me—"

"It doesn't need to occur to you now, either," she said. "I'm just saying, you have a lot. So whatever it is you think you need, maybe you don't need me."

They've been telling us since preschool: *Words hurt*. But I never knew it was actually possible. For words to feel like a slap. To sting with real pain. "You don't mean that."

You can't mean that, I meant. *Please*.

"Okay then, maybe what I mean is that I don't need you."

Somehow, that was almost worse.

And she wasn't done. "Maybe I've got enough going on right now without having to tend to the needs of a spoiled brat who throws a fit every time she doesn't get what she wants."

"Stop it, Marcy, you're just trying to get me mad at you." I knew, of course, what people thought of me. Some people.

Okay, most people.

But she was the one who was supposed to know better. "You're just trying to get me to leave—"

"Yes, you're finally getting it!" she shouted. "At least now we know you're not *stupid* and spoiled. Just spoiled."

"Please stop." I hated how my voice sounded. Weak.

Afraid.

As if I didn't have the nerve to hear what would come next.

Like I said. Words hurt.

"I am trying to get you to leave," she said. Calm now. Not shouting anymore. Not emotional. This was worst of all. "You're right. I do have crap to deal with. And I don't want to tell you about it, okay? I don't want *you* poking your nose into my problems anymore. And I don't want to have to bother pretending I care about yours. So can you just, *please*, leave me alone?"

She was the one who knew all my secrets. The one who knew the ugliest things about me—and loved me anyway. That was the deal with best friends, right? You took off the masks. You showed each other your real faces. You knew that no matter what—no matter how many mistakes you made or how many times you broke the promise to yourself, that you would be nicer, kinder, better—you weren't a monster. You weren't alone. You were someone who could be loved.

But what if the person who knew me best didn't love me after all?

What if she thought I was just as ugly, just as spoiled, just as monstrous, as I'd always secretly feared?

What if she was right?

We stared each other down again, but this time I knew I'd break first. And I had to get out of there before I broke *messy*, all tears and snot and weakness.

So I did. And it's only because after I slammed the door, I sat down on the stoop again—feeling like I couldn't breathe, like I was going to pass out—that I heard her. Marcy. Sobbing.

I thought about it. Opening the door. Forcing her to tell me what was wrong, or maybe just letting her cry without asking any more questions. Letting her call me all the names she wanted, and proving to her that no matter what, I would still be her friend. But I didn't want to be called any more names. I was embarrassed. I was scared going back in would make things even worse.

And, okay, I was out of my mind furious.

Anger was what I did best.

And it always, *always* made me do my worst.

Maybe if I'd stayed, if I'd found a way to make her feel less alone, less helpless, everything would have been different.

But I left.

* * *

At home, I walked straight into an ambush.

Okay, maybe it's not an ambush if somewhere in the back of your mind you knew there was going to be company for dinner. Probably you should have expected the whole happy not-your-family assembled around the dining table staring at you in the doorway like a party crasher. The kind of crasher who ruins everything just by showing up. But the back of my mind was pretty far from the front that night.

"You're two hours late," my mother said. "We were worried sick."

She didn't look worried. She looked furious.

Anger was what my mother did best, too. Add it to the list of crappy things we had in common.

"Daphne, you've grown up so much," Aunt Emma said. Even though I still thought of her that way, *Aunt* Emma, we weren't related. That's just what my mother always called her when I was a little kid. She let me keep calling her that, even after my mother left town.

After my parents split up, Aunt Emma took me out for ice cream and promised she wasn't going to disappear. That we were family. And she must have meant it; every month, she checked in on me, took me out for ice cream, reminded me that she was there if I ever needed her. Some years I saw more of her than I saw of my mother. We never talked about anything important. Sometimes we didn't talk about much at all except what flavor of ice cream to order—but it felt kind of good, imagining my family was a little bigger than just me and my dad. It felt like maybe I wasn't so easy to leave behind as my mother made it seem.

I guess I'd started thinking of Aunt Emma as if she belonged to me. But seeing her with my mother reminded me that they'd belonged to each other first. That maybe she only ever acted like she cared about me because she *actually* cared about my mother. That night, of all nights, the last thing I needed shoved in my face was a reunion between two lifelong best friends.

It was weird to think of Emma and my mother being friends at all, much less best friends—Aunt Emma was round everywhere my mother was sharp, soft everywhere my mother was hard. My mother was a power-suited shark, even here; Emma wore a brown caftan the same color as her frizzy hair. She looked like the kind of woman who baked very good chocolate-chip cookies. Which, I dimly remembered, she did. "It's lovely to see you again," Emma said.

"Yeah. Sure."

Nothing against Aunt Emma. But I couldn't think about anything except Marcy. Those words, *spoiled brat*, were pounding in my head.

"You won't talk to our company that way," my mother said. My stepfather put his hand on hers, like he owned her. That was more than I could take.

"I won't?" I said, not quite yelling, but not quite not. "You're going to tell me what I will and won't do? In my own house? Are you a fortune-teller now? If you can see the future, maybe you can tell me when you're going to vaporize again so I'm not so surprised this time."

"Daphne!" My mother sounded a little like invisible hands were strangling her.

"You're all company, you know," I said. *Spoiled brat. Spoiled brat. Spoiled brat.* "Uninvited guests. So I don't think I have to be very polite after all."

"If you're going to speak that way to us—"

"Oh wait," I said, "maybe I'm psychic now, because I can see exactly what you're going to say, and I agree."

I sent myself to my room. Again. Slammed yet another door. Flung myself on my bed. My queen-sized bed in my own bedroom in my huge house. *Spoiled brat.* Cried my spoiled little eyes out. *Spoiled brat.* With my mother downstairs basically begging me to let her mother me. *Spoiled brat.*

It wasn't true, I thought.

I *wasn't.*

I didn't want to be.

I tried crying myself to sleep, but I was way too hungry for that. So eventually, once it was late and I'd heard the bedroom doors closing, I snuck downstairs, hoping to steal a snack.

Turns out I should have waited a little longer. Aunt Emma and my mother were huddled on the couch together. Something about the way they were sitting made them look younger, like teenagers. Then I realized why—they were sitting the way Marcy and I did, when she was over here. Like best friends. I froze on the stairs, held my breath, listened.

"I'm worried it's my fault," my mother said. "She's had so much, but . . ."

Did she think I was a spoiled brat, too?

She's not allowed to think anything, I reminded myself. She barely knew me.

"She's got a lot of . . . energy," Emma said.

"I just wish she had somewhere to channel it. Something to teach her a little responsibility, teach her the world is bigger than she realizes."

Aunt Emma wrapped her in the kind of warm, comforting embrace I'd never gotten from my mother, and I'd never seen her accept from anyone else. "I have an idea," she said.

And *that* was how I ended up trapped in the town library on a Friday afternoon, pretending that I cared what Aunt Emma's husband, Dr. Thomas Hunter, had in his dusty folders. Old letters, old maps, old newspapers. He kept calling it treasure. Seemed more like dead people's recycling.

My mother had waited till that morning to inform me of my new "job" (no money, of course, so what kind of job was that?). I'd asked whether it was a punishment.

"It's an opportunity," she'd said.

But an opportunity is something you can choose to take or leave. My mother chose for me. As usual.

After an hour, Dr. Hunter left Velma and me alone with our drop-dead-boring work.

"So, what?" I asked Velma. "You actually do this for fun?"

This was stapling. Seriously. Dr. Hunter had set down two gigantic stacks of photocopies between us. I was supposed to take one page from each, hand them to Velma so she could staple them together, and then do it again. And again. And again. Apparently no one had told Dr. Hunter that copy machines could collate and staple themselves. Or maybe torturing his volunteers was just his version of fun.

"Don't talk to me," Velma said. I was impressed she could form words through her gritted teeth.

"Fine."

We worked in silence until my phone buzzed with a call. I would have ignored it, but—

"It's a library," Velma hissed. "You're supposed to turn off your phone."

So, obviously, I had no choice. I answered. Loudly. "Hello?"

"Daffy! What's up, girl?"

It was Nisha Shah, one of those girls I was sort of friends with by default. That's how high school was—if you wore the same kind of clothes and the same kind of makeup and dated the same kind of boys, people just sort of assumed you were friends. It was easiest to let them be right.

Or maybe that's just how I felt.

The older I got, the less sure I was.

"I can't really talk, Nisha." Nisha's dad was in India for two months visiting family, a trip he took every year. For a while now, I'd been wanting to ask Nisha whether it got easier, having him so far away. Whether, when she was a kid and didn't know any better, she'd ever secretly worried he wouldn't come back. Maybe, if we were real friends, she'd be the one person who would actually understand how I felt, having my father on the other side of the planet.

But we weren't real friends. Without Marcy around, I wasn't sure I had any real friends left.

"Just checking if you want a ride to the party tonight," Nisha said.

"What party?"

"Duh. At Shaggy's. It's going to be epic."

Shaggy's parties were, to be fair, always epic. But the last thing I wanted to do was go to a party. Especially one I'd been planning to hit with Marcy, like usual, before I forgot all about it.

"Come on, Daffy, you have to go—I hear there's gonna be a séance. Marcy's gonna try to introduce us to her ghost!"

"Wait . . . Marcy's going to the party?"

Velma's eyes were boring into me. I turned my back on her, lowered my voice.

"How do you know?" I whispered.

"How do you not know? Aren't you two, like, the same person?"

"Pretend we're not—you sure she's going?"

"Shaggy said no doubt. I just talked to him."

I told myself not to be pathetic. You couldn't force someone to be your friend. Especially someone who thought you were a *spoiled brat.*

On the other hand, there was the crying. Marcy wasn't a crier. Was it really so bad to be worried about your best friend in trouble, even after she'd made it pretty clear she wasn't interested in that label anymore? Did that make me some kind of stalker? Or did it just make me a good person?

I didn't know. But I couldn't just let things end. Not like this.

I turned back to face Velma. Still glaring at me. I knew what it was like to walk away from a friendship, cold turkey. Or to let a friend walk away from you.

Not again, I thought. *Not this time.*

"So? Ride? No ride?" Nisha chirped. "Party? No party? Speak, lady."

"I don't need a ride, but . . . party. Yes. I'm in."

VELMA

YOU KNOW THAT MOMENT in a horror movie when the main character hears some kind of weird scratching and moaning coming from the dark, ominous basement, and she thinks, *Huh, I should go down there and check that out*? And you're watching her tromp down the stairs with a dinky little flashlight, descending toward almost certain death. You're covering your eyes and screaming, no, don't, are you insane, stay where you are, or even better, go hide under the bed and let some other character save the day?

That was me, standing just beyond the floodlights of Shaggy's hulking mansion, steeling myself to go inside and face my doom. And that was also me, the little voice inside my head, screaming that I should turn around before it was too late.

It was too late.

I approached the house, heart sinking ever deeper into stomach. The Rogers estate was the biggest house in town. It had been in Shaggy's family for generations and looked, appropriately, like something you'd only find in a horror movie, the kind of gothic estate with bats in the attic, a mummy in the basement, and a bunch of secret doors and hidden corridors eager to trap you in the dark.

I hadn't been here since I was a little kid. Daphne, Fred, Shaggy, and I used to have sleepovers in the great room—that's what Shaggy's mother called it—and after his parents went to bed, we would creep through the house with flash-lights, hunting for ghosts. I think, secretly, we all expected to find some.

Ghosts would have been preferable to what I expected to find that night when I stepped inside. I'd never been to one of Shaggy's infamous parties, and I would have been more than happy to keep it that way. But Marcy was on the other side of that door, and so I was prepared to force myself through it.

"Like, am I hallucinating?" Shaggy asked when he saw me on the doorstep. "Like, I must be hallucinating, because no way did Velma Dinkley actually show up." He swept his arm in a low, dramatic bow. "Consider me honored."

The house was just as impressive inside as it was out. Lots of marble, shiny wood, some glints of gold. A row of gilt-edged portraits lining the hallway, oil paintings of Rogers forefathers, each bearing Shaggy's distinctive broad forehead and sandy hair.

The Rogerses were the closest thing Crystal Cove had to royalty—they could trace their origins back even farther than my father's family, because Shaggy's great-great-great-whatever grandfather had been the only one of the original settlers to survive the mass vanishing. In fact, he was the one who discovered the vanishing. Back in 1850, he'd gone on an expedition inland in search of gold, and returned a month later to find that everyone he knew was gone. There was only one survivor: Rogers's young son, asleep under a tree. Whatever had happened to the rest of the town, he'd slept through the whole thing. Or so he told his father.

Samuel Rogers, the original, had rebuilt the town from scratch. When the town burned down, it was a Rogers who spearheaded the rebuilding *yet again*, persuading the terrified survivors that the land wasn't cursed, that there was no reason to run away, that they could build a bigger and better Crystal Cove on the ashes. (And not so coincidentally, it was a Rogers who would sell them the lumber.)

Ever since, Rogers men (and some women, though in my opinion, not nearly enough) had been behind the scenes, pulling Crystal Cove's strings. Shaggy's dad, also named Samuel Rogers, was enemy number one in our house, at least according to my mother. He wanted to abolish the zoning laws that made sure any Crystal Cove land sold to outside developers didn't damage the character of the town. "*We* are the character of the town," he'd yelled at my mother, during the last town meeting she'd dragged me to. "It's our choice whether we want our character to be poor and mired in the past or rich and looking toward the future."

My father wasn't a huge fan, either, and liked to joke—back when he joked about things—that Mr. Rogers must have blackmail material on everyone in town, because no man had ever been so good at getting everything he wanted.

Shaggy, somehow, had turned out the opposite of what you might expect from a rich kid born to small-town royalty. He didn't act like Crystal Cove's crown prince. He was popular, of course—he was rich, hot, and threw legendary parties, so how could he not be popular—but he didn't much seem to care about that. Or anything else.

Shaggy showed me where to find the food, where to find the drinks, where to find the dancing. (I tried not to shudder.) When I asked if he knew where to find Marcy, he scowled.

"Trust me, you won't be able to miss her. Anyway—" He slung an arm around my shoulder, pulled me in for a quick hug, almost as if we were friends and he was genuinely happy to see me. "Make yourself at home."

"Where are you going?" I asked as he turned toward the grand staircase.

"Up to my room—got a dog and a pizza waiting for me."

"But you're having a party," I said, confused.

"Yeah. I hate parties."

"Um . . . I hate to ask an obvious question, but . . ."

"Think of it as a public service, man," Shaggy said. "I like to spread the joy. So do me a favor, V? Try to look at least a *little* joyful."

I gave him the biggest, fakest smile I could muster. He laughed, and then hurried upstairs. I was dying to follow. Instead, I veered straight into the heart of adolescent darkness, also known as: party time. It was dark, which was good, because I was dressed all wrong—nothing strappy or sparkly or blousy or hot. I'd known that going in, of course. I was wearing my own personal battle gear—thrift store jeans, an orange hoodie, combat boots. Suffice to say, I didn't exactly fit in.

Also, for the record, I didn't have anything against girls who cared about wearing strappy, sparkly, blousy, hot clothes, or cared about clothes at all, much like I didn't have anything against girls who cared about makeup or dating or skin care or whatever clichéd thing high school girls were supposed to care about these days. I'd read Simone de Beauvoir and Chimamanda Ngozi Adichie and Andi Zeisler, I knew all about third-wave feminism and internalized misogyny. I'd also seen *The Devil Wears Prada*—twice. If a girl wanted to be überfeminine and spend all her time staring in the mirror, comparing lip gloss colors, I didn't have anything against it on general principle.

No, it wasn't girls in general I hated. It was these girls in particular. It was Shawna Foster and Haley Moriguchi and Nisha Shah and Marcy Heller and, that dark queen of the feminine dark arts, Daphne Blake. It was these particular girls, who'd gotten some subsonic message in middle school that they were contractually obligated to make me feel like a walking Ugly Doll, and they'd been doing their job with zeal ever since.

Fortunately, they were all too focused on what they were doing to pay much attention to me. What they were doing: not what I expected, from all those teen movies. Or from all that Monday morning gossip about how "epic" and "wild" and "legendary" that weekend's party had been. Mostly, there were just little clumps of people sitting on couches, talking, munching popcorn. Pretty much what I did on a normal Friday night, except with five people crowded onto one couch.

Fred Jones, not surprisingly, was the exception to the rule, doing cartwheels across the crowded room and flirting with any girl he collided with. None of them seemed to mind, and why would they? Fred was as handsome as he was charming, big and blond and absurdly easygoing. Last I'd heard, he was dating Jacqui Parker, a tattooed senior with a Thunderbird, but that was Fred: He'd dated half the girls in school and probably made out with the other half.

Sometimes I thought I was the only girl in school Fred Jones *hadn't* dated. Not that I thought about this. Not much, at least.

One thing was weird, though. The house was filled with popular kids, but the *most* popular girls, the girls everyone else tried to suck up to and imitate—including my prime target, Marcy Heller—were nowhere to be seen. But it didn't take a detective to suss this one out: Wherever I found the little worker bees, I would find their queen. Not in the living room. Not in the dining room. Not in the great hall or the billiards room or the sun porch or the tea lounge.

Then I stepped into the small room in the far west corner of the house, the one that Shaggy used to call his dad's war room, because it was a room with one couch and about a thousand military artifacts—uniforms, battle maps, dusty old helmets, even a sword supposedly used in the Revolutionary War.

The sword hung on the wall, blade pointing straight down like an arrow, and beneath it: Marcy Heller. Surrounded by all her pathetic acolytes, just like I'd thought. Her eyes were closed, her face in shadow. As I got closer, I realized the girls around her had linked hands, and they all had their eyes closed. Marcy was speaking in a hushed, almost holy voice.

"Great spirits of our Crystal Cove forefathers," she said, face tipped to the ceiling. "We ask your forgiveness for our trespass and our disrespect. For our years of partying on your grave."

Unless there were secretly bodies buried in Shaggy's backyard, I figured she was talking about the town's annual anniversary celebration, coming up in a couple weeks. It used to be a solemn commemoration of the mass disappearance, but these days it was just an excuse for people to sell cheap Haunted Village souvenirs and set off illegal fireworks.

"We want to apologize," Marcy said. "We want to atone for our offenses."

"You don't have to apologize to the dead," I told her, sharply. "But maybe you should say you're sorry to some of the living you've offended. Like my mother."

There were six girls in the circle, including Marcy. They all turned to glare at me, as one.

"You're breaking the circuit," Shawna said.

"Not to mention being a total jerk," Haley said.

They were all here, all the girls who could make me miserable with a single glance—all except for Daphne. I wondered where she was and why she wasn't joined to Marcy's hip, as usual, and then reminded myself that wasn't my concern.

"Give me a break," Marcy said, rising to her feet. "Your mom sucks at her job. She deserves whatever she gets."

"You take that back," I said, aware that I was sounding like a child. Pure white-hot rage had a way of making me regress. So did Marcy.

"Or what, Detective Dinkley?"

I flinched. That was what she and all her little minions had called me when we were kids, thanks to Daphne.

"I know you don't care about lying, Marcy, but how do you not care when your lies hurt actual people? Are you really that heartless?"

This time, she flinched. And for a flicker of a second, it seemed like that might actually have gotten through. Then Marcy snickered. "You know what, *Detective*? You don't have a clue. You never did."

On cue, the other girls started laughing and asking if I was going to try to bust the ghost, and I got out of there before I could make everything worse by letting them see they had any power over me.

I nearly slammed into Daphne on my way out the door. Of course. Because no public humiliation could be complete without her.

"Velma?" she said, with an almost perfect imitation of human concern. "You okay?"

"Like you would care," I spat, and then flung myself out the door, into the blissfully cool, quiet dark.

Remember this, I told myself, *next time you feel sorry for yourself about spending so much time alone. At least when you're alone, when you're invisible, there's no one to laugh in your face. And no one to see you cry.*

DAPHNE

I DIDN'T KNOW ANYTHING about Velma anymore—but I knew that look. The one that said she was only barely holding herself together with Scotch tape and string. The one that said she was seconds from falling apart.

Not my problem.

So why was I so tempted to follow her?

Velma was out there somewhere in the night, needing someone—and Marcy was in here, supposedly, needing someone, too. And unlike Velma, Marcy needed *me.* Whether she knew it or not.

I stayed in the house, closed the front door behind me. Refused to let myself be distracted by the past. Velma was strong. She could handle herself.

Typical Shaggy party, everyone showing off for everyone

else. Laughing extra loud so it would be clear they were having fun. Sometimes I wondered if anyone actually had fun at these things, or if we'd all just gotten really good at pretending. Maybe none of us knew the difference anymore.

I spotted Nisha coming out of the war room, shiny in a gold tank top with lipstick to match. The other girls in our crowd were on her heels, all of them cackling like witches.

No Marcy.

"Finally! You missed an epic takedown," Nisha said when she spotted me. "Would you believe *Detective Dinkley* showed up?"

"I would," I said.

"Okay, but would you believe she showed up in that outfit?" Haley said.

Shawna snickered. "You'd think if she's so keen on being a detective, she could *detect* how to dress for a party."

"Maybe she just likes wearing what she wants to wear," I snapped. "Instead of whatever the internet tells her is cool that week. And give the 'Detective Dinkley' thing a break—we're not kids anymore."

"Why are you getting so pissy?" Shawna asked. "You're the one who gave her that nickname in the first place, remember?"

"Yeah." I remembered all right, and it made me want to puke. I wondered if the thought of Velma and what I'd done to her would ever stop making me so sick. Maybe if she disappeared from the face of the earth.

Which did not help the puking situation.

"Can you guys just tell me if you've seen Marcy? I need to talk to her."

Nisha and Haley rolled their eyes at each other, and I knew what that meant. *Daphne's in a mood, just give her what she wants.*

Spoiled brat, I thought. And everyone knew it.

"Upstairs," they said in unison.

"You're kidding." No one was allowed upstairs at Shaggy's parties. It was the only rule he had.

Nisha shrugged. "You know how Marcy feels about rules."

So I broke the only rule of the night and crept up Shaggy's opulent staircase. At the top was a long corridor lined with doors, all of them closed. I tiptoed down the dark hallway. Total déjà vu: Velma and I used to prowl this same hallway, flashlights lighting our way. Both of us pretending we didn't know Fred and Shaggy were hiding behind the doors, waiting to jump out and scare us. They were awful at hiding—Fred got the giggles, and the smell of Shaggy's pizza always gave him away—but it was fun to pretend we were clueless. Sometimes we let them sneak up on us and we faked some pretty good horror movie screams. Sometimes we snuck up on them, and they shrieked for real. That was the most fun of all.

I shook off the past. Again. There were voices coming from the room at the far end. Shaggy's room. I almost knocked, then thought better of it. One useful skill I did pick up from those old days prowling around with Scooby and the gang: eavesdropping. I pressed my ear to the door, held my breath, listened.

"I don't understand how you can do this." It was Shaggy's voice . . . sounding extremely un-Shaggy-like. "What kind of person are you?"

"You know exactly what kind of person I am." That was Marcy. Which made zero sense. Marcy and Shaggy had barely ever spoken to each other, as far as I knew.

"Yeah, and I thought you were better than this."

"I guess you thought wrong," Marcy said.

"You don't have to be so strong all the time, Marcy. You're allowed to lean on someone."

I recognized Marcy's cruel laugh. "And you think that someone would be *you*? It's true what they say, isn't it: The dog has all the brains in this family."

"Maybe you should, like, scram," Shaggy said, his voice icy.

The doorknob turned. Marcy blew past without seeing me and shot down the hallway like a rocket. I chased her down the stairs, out the front door—one more girl throwing herself at the night, determined to be alone in the dark. This time, I followed.

I caught up with her at the end of the block. She was sitting on the curb, her face in her hands, her shoulders shaking.

Crying, for the second time this week. Marcy, who never cried.

I sat beside her. Said nothing. I wasn't about to screw this up again. She didn't say anything, either. Including *go away*. That seemed like a positive sign.

"I'm not going to ask you what's wrong," I said finally.

"Good."

Dead silence. *Awkward* silence. I could hear her trying to steady her breathing, pull back her tears. Trying to be strong.

"It would be really good if you would just leave me alone," she said.

"I'm not doing that, either." I paused. What would I want to hear if I were her?

Wrong question, Daphne.

Self-centered question.

Because I wasn't her. Okay, so what would *she* need to hear? I took a shot.

"You can say whatever you want to me, Marcy. You can be as mean as you want. I'm still not going to leave you alone. I won't do that to you."

She sighed. Her shoulders were still shaking. I put an arm around them. She let me. Another good sign. I hoped.

"I screwed everything up," she said.

"Not possible."

"I thought I could handle it, and then, everything . . . it was too much."

She sagged against me.

"We'll handle it together," I told her. "Whatever it is. You just have to *tell* me, and we'll fix it."

Marcy turned to face me. Even in the dim streetlight I could see her eyes were red, her face streaked with tears—but she smiled. "I love you, Blake. You know that?"

"Duh." But it helped to hear it out loud.

Marcy jumped to her feet. "I have to go back in there and find Dinkley."

"I think she left."

"Crap. Do you have her cell number?"

"Why would I have Velma Dinkley's number?"

"Okay, never mind, I'll figure it out." Marcy squeezed me into a tight hug. "I have to go fix this."

"Fix *what*?"

"I'll tell you everything in the morning, okay? I promise. Meet me at The Mocha at ten. All secrets revealed. Mochas on me. Deal?"

"But—"

"Please?"

"Whatever you need," I said, and I held her tight, wishing I could hold on forever, knowing I had to let her go do whatever it was she needed to do. "You at least want to tell me what you and Shaggy were fighting about?"

She laughed, and it sounded genuine. I knew then, everything would be okay. "Oh, that? You know how he gets about people going upstairs at his parties. I've never met someone who managed to be so laid-back and so uptight at the same time."

"See, not so hard to answer a question," I told her, and for a second, I thought maybe she'd crack, that we would just solve everything tonight. But this was Marcy: She didn't crack. "Okay," I allowed. "Tomorrow."

"Tomorrow." She said it like a promise.

* * *

I barely slept. When dawn cracked the sky, I finally let myself get out of bed. This still left hours to kill, and I murdered each one of them slowly and painfully, waiting out the morning.

I got to The Mocha early, gulped down more coffee than I should have, planned what I was going to say. Or, because that was mostly impossible, given that I couldn't imagine what *she* was going to say, planned how I was going to react. Whatever she told me, I promised myself, I wouldn't flinch. I wouldn't judge, I wouldn't freak out, I wouldn't do whatever she must be worrying I would do.

Most of all, I wouldn't make it about myself. Marcy had been keeping secrets from me for a reason. I would prove to her that the reason, whatever it was, had been wrong. That I was her best friend, and I could be a good one.

By ten o'clock, I was ready.

No Marcy.

Fifteen minutes passed. No Marcy. I startled every time the door swung open. Deflated every time it wasn't her.

Then another half hour passed. No Marcy.

Finally, I stopped staring at the door. *When she's an hour late*, I told myself, *I'll leave.*

I drank mug after mug of coffee. I waited. I fumed. I felt like Charlie Brown with the stupid football, falling for this again and again.

I swore I wouldn't pathetically text and call Marcy to find out what had happened. Then I texted, called, texted again, pointlessly.

Finally, half the day wasted on waiting—and the rest of the weekend, I already knew, doomed to be wasted on wondering—I accepted the obvious. She wasn't coming. She'd ghosted me. She didn't care that she'd promised me, she didn't care that I was worrying about her. She must not have cared, period, or she wouldn't act the way she did.

What did it say about me, I thought—once I finally gave up on her, paid the bill, walked out alone—that the person I cared about most in the world didn't care about me at all?

And what did it say about me that even then, I still wanted her to?

* * *

I had the whole weekend to be seriously pissed off. It didn't help that my house was still filled with intruders, and I was in no mood to pretend otherwise. I wanted to rage. To tell them to get out. I *really* wanted to pick another fight with my mother. Or maybe wage a small thermonuclear war on her.

But there was that annoying voice in the back of my head. The one saying every time I yelled at her, I felt worse about myself. Especially when I did it in front of the step-brats. It always made them cry. And I almost always did it in front of the step-brats, because wherever I went, there they were.

So I shut myself in my room. Saturday, I worried. Sunday, I forced myself to stop. It wasn't like Marcy was worrying about me, I reminded myself. So why waste the energy? Why not just think about myself? That's what she expected of me. What everyone expected of me. Spoiled, sullen, self-centered Daphne Blake, right? Even my own mother clearly thought that, deep down. So why not prove them right?

Sunday night: still pissed. Monday morning: *more* pissed. I showed up at school ready to tell her off.

So you can imagine how pissed I was when she didn't show up. Pissed at Marcy for cutting, again, pissed at myself for caring, still. Pissed straight through till the moment I got called out of fifth period, summoned to the principal's office, where Shaggy's mom was waiting. Except she wasn't there as Shaggy's mom—she was in uniform.

No one would ever say it to Shaggy's face, but we all thought it was kind of weird that his mom was a cop. His dad basically pulled all the strings in Crystal Cove—and no one thought he pulled them, well, *legally*. But Lieutenant Rogers had been a cop when they met, and she stayed that way. My dad thought it was her way of giving back. Marcy thought it was her way of smoothing the way for her shady husband. Personally, I didn't see why it had to be one or the other.

Anyway, she was a cop. And she was in school on official business. Lieutenant Rogers, reporting for duty—and that duty was obviously me.

Maybe some part of me had known. Maybe, beneath all that being pissed, what I really was, was terrified.

She shook my hand, tried halfheartedly to smile. "It's been a while, Daphne. You're all grown up."

"Is this about Marcy?"

She looked weirdly satisfied. "Why would you assume that?"

"Can you just tell me what's going on?"

"I gather you and Marcy Heller are very close."

I nodded. If that's what she'd heard, I didn't see any reason to offer a more recent update.

"When's the last time you saw her?"

I could barely breathe. "Friday. Why?"

"Did she mention any upcoming intention to leave town?"

"No. *Why?*"

"I'm sorry to have to tell you this, Daphne, but your friend Marcy is missing."

"Missing?" It came out as a squeak. "Like, *kidnapped*? Or . . ." I didn't want to think about any *ors*. I couldn't.

"Judging from the email she sent her parents, it looks like she ran away." Her voice hardened. "Would you know anything about that, Daphne?"

"What? No, of course not."

"She's your best friend, right?"

I nodded.

Shaggy's mother smiled an extremely fake smile. I felt like a suspect, but I had no clue what she suspected me of. "I remember being your age, having a best friend. We told each other everything. All our secrets, all our problems. All our big plans. Is that the kind of friendship you and Marcy have?"

I nodded. Not like it was any of her business what kind of friendship we had. Or didn't have. Or used to have. I no longer knew.

"So she wouldn't have run away without telling you *something*, right? Why she left, where she was going . . ."

"Exactly! Which is why I know she didn't run away."

"You're not doing her any favors, keeping her secrets. This is serious, Daphne. She could be in trouble."

"I know it's serious," I insisted. "And she *is* in trouble, because I'm telling you, there's no way she ran away on her own."

Not without telling me first. Not without saying goodbye. And especially not the morning after she swore she was ready to confide in me, that we were going to fix everything together. It wasn't possible.

"As I understand it, Marcy's been going through a difficult time lately," Lieutenant Rogers said. "Cutting school, breaking up with her boyfriend—"

"Something bigger was going on with her," I admitted. "I don't know what—I'm not lying about that, I swear. But I'm telling you, she was in trouble. Not the kind of trouble you run away from."

"How do you know that if you don't know what it was?" Lieutentant Rogers sounded skeptical.

"What if you're wrong?" I said. "If she didn't run away, then it means someone *took* her away."

Lieutenant Rogers sighed. She wasn't looking at me like I was a suspect anymore. She was looking at me like she felt sorry for me because I was a clueless idiot. "She emailed her parents to tell them she was leaving, Daphne. And we've searched her computer—there's evidence indicating she was planning to go to Mexico."

"No way. I don't believe it. *Something* happened to her." But I could tell, even as I was talking, that it was pointless. She was barely listening to me. I was just some hysterical girl refusing to face reality. *How sad*, she probably thought. Poor little rich girl gets abandoned by everyone she loves. Still can't wrap her head around the idea that her best friend would ditch her without a word. Needs to invent some ridiculous kidnapping theory just to make herself feel better.

One of us was dead wrong. I just wished I was more sure which one.

"Her parents don't seem worried about that possibility," Lieutenant Rogers said.

I laughed humorlessly. "Marcy's parents have never bothered to worry about anything Marcy-related."

"It seems to me that's all the more reason for her to run away," she replied. "Unhappy teens act out. Be grateful you don't understand."

What I did understand was that Marcy was in trouble. I knew it, deep down. It was easy to feel uncertain about myself, but I was certain of Marcy Heller.

I knew her. I knew what she'd do, how she'd act, if she'd decided to run away, and it wasn't like this. I *wanted* to be wrong, because then she'd be okay.

But something else was going on, I was sure—something worse. And if I was the only one who realized it, maybe that made me the only one who could save her.

VELMA

A LESSON MY GRANDMOTHER had drilled into me from birth: If it seems too good to be true, it probably is.

TO: JinkiesDinkleys

FROM: MarcyHellcat

You were right about me. You were right about everything. But I'm going to fix it. I swear. Call as soon as you get this.

Also.

I'm sorry.

The message was waiting for me when I woke up Saturday morning—if you can call it "waking up" when all you did all night was toss and turn and get trapped in nightmares about the world's most humiliating party.

So maybe I was a little bleary-eyed, a little off my game,

and that's why I forgot lesson number one. I got suckered into thinking, if only for a few minutes, that Marcy Heller actually had a soul. Then I called the number she gave me. It went straight to voice mail. And like a huge sucker, I actually believed she would call me back. Or respond to my messages. Or do anything except ghost me. I didn't understand exactly what the joke was supposed to be, but one thing was clear: The joke was on me.

That's what I thought until Monday, at least, when word went around school that Marcy had left town. So maybe she wasn't pranking me after all? Maybe she'd had a genuine moment of remorse . . . but instead of actually dealing with her crap, she just ran away like a scared little girl. I didn't think it was possible to be any angrier. But the idea of her skipping across the country with her parents' credit cards, having herself a nice little vacation, while my mother got fired and we ran out of money and maybe a place to live and I couldn't even think about what might happen after that? It made me sick with rage. At least while Marcy was *here*, there was still a chance she would finally tell the truth. If she'd disappeared, then there was no way to counter her story. And probably people would say it was whatever had happened in the Haunted Village that made her run. My mother would seem even more negligent. Just by leaving, she'd managed to make things worse.

By lunchtime I was fuming, and the last thing I needed

was a dose of Daphne Blake. Especially a Daphne who'd invaded my own personal turf, the shady hiding spot where I could usually count on eating in peace. It takes a certain amount of energy to be polite when you're seething with rage, and I had no energy left to spare.

"This is my spot," I told her.

"Oh really? Where's the sign?" She feigned searching in confusion, then shrugged. "Nope, nothing that says 'reserved for losers.'"

It also takes a certain amount of energy to fight back. Instead, I gave her the finger and turned away. There were plenty of other trees, other hidden nooks. I'd find an easier one.

"Wait!" Daphne said, and something in her voice made me hesitate. "I'm sorry. I get mean when I'm upset."

"Yeah. No kidding."

"Just sit down. There's space here for both of us. Or . . . I'll go. If you want. Whatever."

She looked sincerely sorry. Also . . . incredibly sad. I sighed. I sat.

"Guess you heard about Marcy," she said, sagging back against the sturdy tree trunk.

"Yeah, I heard." Our town didn't have much space for secrets.

"You must be thrilled."

"Excuse me?"

"Oh, come on, Velma. You hate her, and now, *poof*, she's gone. It must feel like Christmas."

"You're kidding me, right?" I'd been aiming for polite, because I knew Daphne—for whatever incomprehensible reason—actually *cared* about Marcy. Was probably distraught at being ditched for the open road. But that didn't excuse her being this oblivious. "Marcy makes up some insane story about the Haunted Village and tries to get my mom fired, just for fun—she made a huge mess of my life and she's the one person who could clean it up. So when I finally manage to hammer that into her thick head, and she swears to me she's going to do it, what does she do? She runs away and leaves her lies behind, to just sit and rot. And you think I'm *thrilled*?"

"What do you mean, she swore she was going to clean up her mess?"

I showed her the message Marcy had sent me, the useless promise with its equally useless apology. "I thought it was a nasty joke," I said. "But now I'm thinking she just chickened out."

Daphne shook her head. "No. This is for real. She said almost the same thing to me, after the party—that she wanted to find you, fix things. And I know she meant it."

"How?"

"I just . . . I know her," Daphne said, and sniffed the way you do when you're trying very hard not to cry.

I reminded myself not to feel sorry for her. This was, after all, Daphne Blake. My enemy. "If you know her so well, did you know she was going to run away?"

Daphne took a deep breath. "If I tell you something, will you try to take it seriously? Like, not laugh at me or tell me I'm being stupid or overly emotional or something?"

"No promises. But . . ." The thing about enemies is that it's a lot harder to hate them when they're sitting right in front of you looking like they're about to fall apart. "Look, it's obviously been a long time since we actually knew each other, or whatever. But the Daphne I used to know was never stupid. Or overly emotional. So just say it."

"I don't think she ran away. I think something happened to her."

"What?"

Daphne told me about Marcy breaking down at Shaggy's party, then flaking out on their coffee shop date the next morning—and then, like her internal floodgates finally burst, she told me everything else, about how Marcy'd been acting weird and evasive for the last couple months, how it was starting to feel like she had a whole secret life. "And then, just when she's finally ready to tell me everything, she . . . what? Walks out of her life?" Daphne shook her head. "It doesn't make any sense. And don't even get me started on the email she supposedly sent her parents."

"No, get started," I urged her, substantially more curious than I wanted to be.

"Okay, according to the cops, it basically said, *Dear Mom and Dad, I'm leaving town. Don't bother to look for me. Don't blame yourselves. I love you.* And when they checked her browser history, which I guess they do when you disappear—"

"Good to know," I murmured.

"—they found all these searches for Baja surfing towns and bus schedules to Mexico."

"Marcy ran away to *Mexico*? That's hard to picture."

"It's impossible to picture," Daphne said. "That's my point. First of all, Marcy hates hot weather and she hates the beach even more, so why would she ever run away to Mexico? Second of all, even if she did, she'd only be doing it to piss off her parents and get them to notice her."

"Why do you say that?"

"Because that's the only reason Marcy ever does anything," Daphne said. "So why would she tell them not to blame themselves? Getting them to blame themselves would be the whole point."

"You think someone else wrote that email," I realized.

"Yes."

"And that same someone got on her computer, set up the Mexico searches to be found. Red herrings."

Daphne rolled her eyes. It was mildly impressive how even in panic mode she could still take a break to make sure I felt suitably inferior. "That's what I'm *saying*."

"You think someone . . ." I didn't even want to say it. This wasn't an imaginary ghost hunt in Shaggy's attic, and it wasn't a search for Fred's little brother's missing turtle. This was a real mystery—and, if Daphne was right, a really dangerous one. "You think someone took her."

She hesitated, and I knew she didn't want to say it, either. She probably didn't even want to think it. But she clearly couldn't help herself. "Yes."

"What did the cops say?"

"That I'm 'overly emotional.' Translation, young and stupid."

"And female," I added.

"Yeah," she said bitterly. "That too. They sent me to the guidance counselor, like that's going to help. And meanwhile, her parents are sending the cops and some kind of high-priced private investigator to *Mexico.* What happens to Marcy while everyone's wasting time looking for her in the wrong place?"

"Not everyone," I said.

"What do you mean?"

"Not you," I pointed out. "If you're right about this, then she'll have *you* looking for her, hopefully in the right place."

"I'm sixteen years old. How exactly am I supposed to do better than the cops? Or a private detective?"

My brain started to buzz with the puzzle of it, and I couldn't help myself. "The logical place to start would be her apartment, right?" I suggested. "Look for clues, anything that might tip you off to what actually happened? You said she's been acting weird for a while—maybe you can find something at her place that will explain why?"

Daphne looked like she was buzzing, too. "Can we go right after school?"

"Uh . . . *we*?"

She looked as surprised as I felt, and I wondered if she'd even meant to say it. "Well, yeah. We."

For one dangerous second, I felt like we were kids again, back in the mystery van, plotting how to solve our next case. Daphne and Velma, unstoppable, unbreakable. So I'd thought.

I shook off the memory. I'd been a foolish kid to put my faith in her or in anything. It wasn't a mistake I'd let myself make again. "How did this become a *we* situation?"

"You want to find her as much as I do," Daphne said. "She can clear your mom, right? Find Marcy, find the truth."

She had a point. A huge one.

"I still think she ran away, probably because she was afraid of getting in trouble," I said, unsure if I actually believed it.

"Okay, so prove it. If not for your mom, then for you."

"What's that supposed to mean?"

Daphne broke into a smile, and it turned her face into sunshine. "Like you said, it's obviously been a long time since we knew anything about each other, but the Velma I knew? She'd do anything to prove herself right."

* * *

So I went with her to Marcy's apartment. Because I wanted to track down Marcy, one way or another. Because if Daphne was correct, it was the right thing to do. Because I was curious. Because I didn't want to deprive myself of the opportunity to be proven right. And maybe because, even after all these years, when Daphne Blake needed me, I couldn't say no.

It had been such a long time since she'd needed me.

If I'm gong to be really honest, it had been a long time since anyone had needed me.

Not all apartments are created equal. Ours was a dump, a dingy concrete box nestled inside a bigger dingy concrete box. Marcy's apartment complex looked more like a hotel, or at least a very fancy motel—there was a mirrored lobby, a community garden, even a pool. Daphne retrieved the spare key Marcy had hidden under a fake brick on the edge of the community garden. "She told me where it was, in case of emergencies," Daphne said, hesitating at Marcy's doorstep. "I never thought I'd actually use it. She's pretty intense about her privacy."

"If you're right, this is an emergency," I reassured her. "She'd want you to help her."

"*Want* is a strong word," Daphne said. "All Marcy ever wants is to handle things herself."

It seemed sad, for both of them. But it also seemed totally understandable. "Okay then, she *needs* you to help her."

Daphne turned the key. I gasped. Marcy's apartment looked like a tornado had ripped through it—clothes flung everywhere, drawers and cabinets yawning open, pots and pans overturned, old magazines scattered across the kitchen floor. "You think the cops did this?" I asked, shocked. "Or . . . whoever took her?"

Daphne looked around, confused. "Did what?"

"You know . . ." I swept out an arm to encompass the general disarray, and Daphne laughed.

"Oh, that's just Marcy. What would your place look like if you lived on your own?"

It would probably look exactly the same as it did now: books alphabetized on shelves, bed made with hospital corners, dust vanquished from every surface.

"Oh," Daphne said, with a smile that indicated she was remembering what she knew about me. "Right."

"Let's just start looking around, see if we can find anything useful."

"What do you think we're looking for?"

"You'll know it when you see it." I hoped I sounded more confident than I felt. "You know her best of anyone, so you'll know if anything seems off."

Daphne gave me a quick, awkward hug, then backed away like she was afraid it might provoke violence.

"What was that for?" I asked.

"Just . . . thanks. For coming here with me. Even if you don't believe me."

"I don't traffic in beliefs," I reminded her. "I wait for facts. Let's find some."

While Daphne poked, with obvious squeamishness, through Marcy's belongings, I wandered the apartment, trying to imagine the girl who lived here. Not the Marcy Heller I knew from school, but the private one, the person she became when no one was watching. I wondered if she liked it here, on her own, her parents hopping all over the globe having adventures without her. My parents didn't even like to leave me alone for a weekend—they would never have just moved away and left me behind. I would never have wanted them to. It was hard to believe that Marcy had any actual emotions other than meanness, but maybe feeling mean came easier than feeling lonely, or abandoned.

I poked around Marcy's desk, which looked like it hadn't been cleaned in a decade and smelled like she'd spilled a whole bottle of perfume on top of the clutter. Which made it easy to notice the one neat, tidy corner, piled with a stack of printouts. I flipped through them—they were reports of recent real estate deals in Crystal Cove, along with pages of business listings and corporate websites, all for California real estate developers and law firms. I recognized one of them—it was Daphne's stepfather's firm, the one that had helped take away my home.

"Daphne, is there any reason Marcy would have been researching real estate? Or development companies and their law firms?"

"Like the crap my dear old stepfather George does?" Daphne shook her head. "No way. Marcy could barely be bothered to research a recap of her favorite show when she missed an episode."

"Huh." Interesting.

I decided Marcy wouldn't mind if I took the papers home for future consideration, and tucked them into my bag. One escaped, and when I knelt to grab it, I noticed the floor was covered with crushed yellow flower blossoms, which was weird, because there were no flowers in sight, not even a vase. I picked one up, smelled it—sickly sweet. I pocketed one of the blossom fragments, too, just in case.

Then I moved on to the kitchen. Oven: filled with folded sweaters and jeans. Fridge: empty. She'd turned the front of the refrigerator into a collage of photos, almost all of them selfies of Daphne and Marcy—lounging in the school parking lot, dancing in the apartment, peering into the darkness of the sea caves with mock horror. In some of them, they looked like the Daphne and Marcy I knew in school, hair and makeup picture-perfect, clothes runway ready. But in others they were in their pajamas, in workout sweats, in face masks—not performing for anyone but each other.

It really hit me then. These were the kinds of goofy photos

you took with your best friend. The kinds of photos Daphne and *I* used to take, when we were best friends, which I still had in a shoebox under my bed that I never allowed myself to open. I wondered: If that one terrible summer hadn't blown up our friendship, would it be me in these pictures, instead of Marcy?

The thought of it, of how easily Daphne had just slotted someone else into my place, while I'd spent all these years alone, should have made me angry. Under any other circumstance, maybe it would have. But here, in the apartment Marcy had left behind, with Daphne desperately prowling through her best friend's life and pretty obviously trying not to have a total meltdown, it just made me sad. I had spent so much time hating Daphne that I'd forgotten—or maybe I forced myself to forget—what a good friend she could be. Loyal. Tough. Smart. Determined, always, to make things okay. Watching her miss Marcy made me, for the first time in years, miss Daphne.

When Daphne finished her search, we sat down on the front stoop—the cleanest surface we could find—to go through what she'd uncovered.

"This is her secret cash stash," Daphne said, showing me a wad of bills stuffed into a tampon box. "She said that statistically, most home invasions are done by men, and if there's one thing dudes avoid like the plague, it's tampons."

"Smart," I admitted.

"Too smart to run off to Mexico without it," Daphne said, and I had to agree.

Then she showed me a piece of turquoise sea glass, the size of her palm and the color of the ocean on a perfect, sunny day. "She's had this since she was a little kid," Daphne said. "She found it with her dad on the only vacation he ever took her on. It's her prized possession."

"So, again, why would she leave without it?"

"Exactly. Okay, her wallet is gone, some of her clothes and a suitcase are gone, the cops told me that. But not her favorite clothes—those are all still here. Are you telling me she'd run away with the hideous wool turtleneck her aunt gave her last Christmas but she'd leave behind the denim jacket she only bought after she'd tried on every single denim jacket in a fifty-mile radius so she could get the absolute perfect fit? Does that make sense to you?"

"Almost nothing that just came out of your mouth made sense to me," I admitted, though I suspected I didn't mean it the way she did.

"The only things missing from this apartment are the kind of things a stranger would pack if they were trying to make it look like she left in a hurry. And also—"

She showed me something on the doorjamb, something smudged and red.

"This stain wasn't here the last time I came," Daphne said. "And am I wrong, or does it look kind of like . . ."

"Blood?"

"I'm scared, V. What if . . ."

I stood up. Then took her hands, pulled her to her feet. I wasn't going to let her fall apart. Not on my watch. "Okay, here's the plan. We go to the police with all this, and hope they want to listen this time. Or her parents, if they won't. We try to get someone to hear you."

"And if they won't? If they just blow me off for being some dumb kid?"

"Then we find her ourselves."

"Did you say . . . *we*?" Daphne said, a tremble in her voice like she was just waiting for me to tell her she'd heard wrong.

"*We*," I repeated.

Daphne threw her arms around me and pulled me into a tight hug, and this time there was nothing awkward about it. It felt more right than I wanted it to. It felt a little like coming home.

"We'll look for her, and we'll keep looking until we find her," I murmured. "I promise."

It is a night ripe for haunting. The moon hides behind the clouds, as if it knows better than to show its face on a night like this. There are no stars. There is nothing above or below to witness the man leaning against a thick tree trunk, gazing up at a leafy canopy, reminding himself he does not believe in ghosts.

He should not be here.

He should not be here tonight, steeling himself to ascend a rickety ladder, to install a cheap security camera, on the branches of a tree that has stood guardian over this land for centuries. He should not be in this job, doing shoddy maintenance work for a tourist trap. He should not be in this town, three thousand miles from any soul who might care if he lives or dies.

But here he is, nonetheless.

Here tonight because his very competent manager has been suspended and the incompetent man taking her place cannot read a shift schedule and could not find it in himself to care whether an employee had already worked three overnights in a row. Here at all because he is a poet, and man cannot pay rent by poetry alone. Here for good because his allergies drove him to it, to exile himself somewhere with dry air and clean skies. Although tonight—

Aaaaaaah-CHOOO!

Tonight is also a night ripe for pollen. Every breath he takes is labored, blossom sweet. Every exhale a sneeze deferred.

He leans the ladder against the tree. Apologizes to the tree.

While he does not believe in ghosts, he believes in respect. This tree was planted by the original settlers of Crystal Cove, the men and women who'd left their homes in search of a brighter future, built homes and families in this new world, until, one day, they vanished. Beneath this tree, hundreds of years ago, the lone survivor had been found: A young boy, asleep, awakened to discover everyone he loved was gone.

Next week, beneath this tree, now known as the Vanishing Tree, the people of Crystal Cove will come together in commemoration and celebration of those original settlers. And of the money their disappearance continues to generate for the descendants of those who have replaced them.

The man cares about none of this. He cares only about the fact that he has to climb a ladder. And he is afraid of heights.

He ascends, one step at a time. Refuses to look at the ground wobbling beneath him. Tries not to sneeze. Tries to ignore the whispers on the wind, which are not whispers, because there is no such thing as ghosts.

Beware . . .

The wind seems to say.

Above him, something bright flickers through the leaves. Something like eyes.

A squirrel, he tells himself, and reminds himself to breathe. Stay steady. Hold on. Do not look at the eyes. Do not fall for the illusion of a gaping mouth, opening in the darkness, speaking with the voice of the wind, bewarebewarebewarebeware.

He says, aloud, "No." *He lets the camera fall to the ground, break into pieces. He holds on to the ladder, afraid to go down, afraid to stay up. Afraid.*

This is our land, *the ghost says.* You will not mock us on our own land, *and it is a ghost, it is a blur of infinite darkness swooping toward him, it is shadow hands reaching for him, and he reminds himself to hold on and stay steady but the maw of darkness is opening for him and every muscle in his body screams for escape, what can he do but recoil, let go, fall*

and fall

and fall

forever, into the black.

DAPHNE

IT FELT WRONG BRINGING Velma to The Mocha. That was our place, mine and Marcy's. Bringing anyone would have felt like a betrayal. But Velma? That's the one betrayal Marcy wouldn't have been able to stand. It felt like an admission that she wasn't coming back.

But that's why we were here, I reminded myself: *for* Marcy. To get her back.

We were also here because Aunt Emma and Dr. Hunter—his name was Thomas, but he just didn't seem like the kind of guy you could call anything but *Dr.*—had invited me and Velma over for what would probably be the world's most boring dinner. The Mocha was down the street from their house. Which made it the perfect place to meet beforehand and compare notes on what Velma called our *theories of the crime.* One problem: Neither of us had come up with any good theories.

After we checked out Marcy's apartment, we'd called Lieutenant Rogers and tried to explain the evidence we found. By which I mean, we tried to make her believe it was *evidence.* She didn't want to hear it. She even had the nerve to be mad at *us* for trespassing.

"I don't think you understand," I said, trying not to let the anger swell out of me and into the phone.

"I don't think *you* understand," she retorted. "This kind of meddling isn't helping anyone. Not you, and certainly not your friend. You're just getting in the way."

"In the way of what? You not bothering to do your job?"

I guess it shouldn't have been a shock when she hung up on me.

We'd spent the next two days trying everything we could think of to persuade someone to listen to us. I called Marcy's parents. No luck. I even got them to put me in touch with the private investigator they'd hired, and that guy was thrilled to talk to me . . . right up to the moment he realized I knew nothing whatsoever about Marcy's plans to run away to Mexico, except that they were total fiction. He didn't want to hear it, either.

After that, Velma and I figured we were on our own. Apparently being under the age of eighteen meant we had a neon sign hanging over our heads that said TOTALLY USELESS.

"The adult world is almost wholly populated by people secretly terrified someone's going to figure out they have no idea what they're doing," Velma told me. "If they allowed themselves even thirty seconds to imagine two teenagers knew more than they did? They'd lose their minds."

I knew she was just trying to make me feel better.

It worked.

Now, in The Mocha, we were launching a new strategy. A DIY strategy. Mission *Find Marcy, totally on our own*. Neither of us mentioned what had happened the last time we decided to start our own little detective agency, but I had a feeling we were both thinking about it.

"First we should make a list of Marcy's enemies," Velma suggested.

"But she doesn't have any enemies."

Velma raised her eyebrows. "You're kidding, right?"

Okay, yes, Marcy wasn't exactly sugar and spice and anything nice. "I'm talking real enemies," I told Velma. "Maybe a lot of people hate her, but no one who would, like, *do* anything about it. I mean, you hate her, right?"

Velma hesitated, then—because there was no point in arguing—nodded.

"But you don't want to kidnap her or anything, right?"

"Obviously not."

"Exactly. And trust me, I wish there was someone obvious," I admitted. "Because if not . . ."

"If not . . . ?"

"The more random a crime is, the harder it is to solve," I said. "If some stranger just—" I stopped. Couldn't bring myself to think any further down that path. Of course, all I'd been doing since Marcy vanished was thinking further and further down that path.

"That's true," Velma said, and she sounded a little impressed that I'd thought of it. "But whatever happened, it doesn't sound random—you said yourself that she'd started acting strangely, keeping secrets, right?"

"Right."

"And she admitted that something was going on, something too big for her to handle? Just before she disappeared, right?"

"Right."

"So it would be pretty coincidental if those two things weren't connected."

"Right!" I'd told myself all this, too, but it was more persuasive hearing it from someone else. I was too emotionally invested. Velma hated her enough to be objective, and right now, that was exactly what Marcy needed. "So we should trace her activities, try to figure out what she's been doing."

"That's exactly what I was going to suggest!" Velma said.

"Don't laugh," I said, and pulled a purple notebook out of my bag, flipped it open to the first page. "But I started a case notebook for us, just like we used to."

Velma flinched, and I wondered if I'd gone too far, mentioning the past. Then she reached into her bag and pulled out an identical notebook. Grinned. When she flipped hers open to the first page, I burst into laughter. We'd both written exactly the same thing:

TALK TO TREY

Marcy's boyfriend, at least until recently. The obvious place to start.

"You think he'll talk to you?" Velma asked.

"We should talk to him together," I said. "Just in case he knows anything and intends to lie about it. You'll throw him off balance."

"How will I do that?"

"You don't have to do anything, just be you," I said. "He's intimidated by you."

She looked at me like I was speaking in a foreign language. *"Why?"*

"Um, a ton of people are intimidated by you." I decided not to mention that one of them was me. "Especially guys." She still looked confused—maybe even more so. "Look, for one thing you're stealth hot. Like, the kind of hot they maybe don't even consciously notice, but some part of their brain registers it, and that just leaves them incredibly confused."

"Thank you . . . I think?"

"And you're also super smart, obviously. And tough. You don't care what anyone thinks of you, which is a big one, and it's pretty obvious you don't need anything or anyone. You're totally self-contained. That intimidates people. It makes them respect you. Seriously . . . you must know that?"

Velma was blinking super fast, her face getting redder and redder. Maybe she didn't know it after all.

She tugged at her turtleneck. "That's not really how I think of myself."

"Maybe you should start," I suggested.

That's when things got awkward. Or more awkward, at least. I wasn't sure what I'd said wrong, but I was pretty sure I wasn't supposed to notice that her blushing was going nuclear. Unfortunately, there was nowhere else to look.

Lucky for both of us, Velma was still Velma: She got it together, and then got us back to business. "So, should we talk about the other issue?" she said, brisk and efficient.

"What other issue?"

"The second ghost sighting," she said.

I snorted.

"I guess that means you heard?" she said.

The whole town had heard. The *Howler* had blasted the headline all over the internet, so probably the whole planet had heard. Crystal Cove was getting more famous—and apparently more haunted—by the day. What a joke. "What, that some maintenance dude got drunk at work, fell off a ladder, and broke his leg? And now he's crying 'ghost'? Yeah, I heard."

"I know Sameer," Velma said, sounding pissed. "There's no way he was drunk at work. And I don't think he's lying about what he saw."

I gaped at her, incredulous. "You're not telling me you believe in ghosts now?"

"Of course not! I don't believe he saw a ghost, but I believe *he* might believe it."

"Oh, I get it—you were so sure Marcy's just a big, fat liar. But this random guy must be telling the truth?"

It felt like our temporary truce was very close to exploding in our faces. I didn't care. There was so much emotion bubbling inside me—so much terror and guilt and rage. For a moment, I let myself imagine how good it would feel to just vomit it all out, even if it landed in a steaming heap on Velma's lap.

"I'm saying maybe they both saw something," Velma explained, and my boil cooled back down to a simmer. I hated feeling this close to the edge, this close to exploding. But the worse things got, the harder it was to back away. "A second ghost sighting, in the same location? It seems like it must be connected, right?"

She was right. Of course she was right. She was Velma.

Before I could tell her so, some girl I barely knew—I wasn't even sure if her name was Cassie or Casey—rushed over to our table and threw her arms around me.

"Daphne! Oh my gosh, I saw you over here and I have to tell you I'm so, so sorry about Marcy! It's nuts, right? Have you heard from her? Do you know where she is? Are you just, like, freaking out?"

"Uh, I'm okay." I disentangled myself. From the corner of my eye, I could see Velma trying very, very hard not to laugh.

"Marcy's just the *best*, you know?"

I wanted to ask her if she'd ever even spoken to Marcy. I wanted to ask her what made her think she knew anything about either of us, and why she was suddenly so desperate to latch on to me like some kind of misery vampire. But I was afraid if I opened my mouth, I'd bite her head off.

"We're kind of busy here, Carrie," Velma said.

The girl—*Carrie*, apparently—turned to Velma for the first time, and made a face like she smelled something terrible. "Are you, like, implying something?" she asked.

"No, I'm spelling it out," Velma said. "You're interrupting us." She put on a syrupy fake, chirpy voice. "So have a nice night! Somewhere else!"

Carrie's jaw dropped wide open, like I'd only seen in cartoons. "You can't—" She looked at me, found no support. "Whatever." Then she stalked away.

I burst into laughter. "I love you, V." It came out before I realized what I was saying, but fortunately Velma was laughing too hard to hear.

"What *was* that?" Velma sputtered.

"It's been happening for days," I told her. "The only thing worse is the people who don't say anything at all. They just stare at me with these big, watery eyes, like, *Oh, poor Daphne, you must be so worried and so sad*. That's what my mother keeps doing. Like she's afraid I'm going to run away next. My dad, too—he offered to come home from Japan, can you believe it?"

"Did you take him up on it?" Velma asked. I'd told her about my family situation, the whole absentee-dad, unasked-for-mom thing, but not how I felt about it. I suspected she had enough clues to crack that case herself.

"I was so tempted, but." *But* I couldn't let him do it, give up his dream, just because he thought I needed him. I did need him—but not any more than I had a week ago, or any other day of my life. "It's all I've been wishing for, you know? That he would just up and decide to come home. Having it happen now, like this? It's like I somehow wished Marcy gone."

"That's magical thinking," Velma said. "You know that, right? You can't feel guilty for *thinking* things—and last I checked, you can't control the universe with your brain."

"I wish I could. I'd think Marcy right home again."

"And that's the other reason you shouldn't feel guilty," Velma said. "So let's just do it."

"What?"

"Think her home. Come up with a strategy. That's why we're here, right?" She took a sip of her mocha, made a face. "It's definitely not for the quality of the coffee."

"It's an acquired taste," I admitted. The timer I'd set on my phone dinged. I sighed. "We should go to this dinner thing. Unless you've got some genius idea for getting us out of it?"

Velma rolled her eyes. "If only."

"Why don't you want to go?" I asked her. "You love Dr. Dull-as-Dirt."

"He's not dull," she snapped. "I just wish he'd married someone a little less . . . touchy-feely."

"He's *lucky* someone like Emma agreed to marry him," I argued. "She's amazing."

"She's very nice," Velma granted. "She's just, I don't know. She's very into, like, elaborate centerpieces. And hugging."

I remembered only now how much Velma hated people hugging her. "I guess it's true, opposites attract," I said, shrugging.

I almost wondered if I was talking about them, or about us.

* * *

I'd been to Aunt Emma's house a few times when I was a kid, but it was smaller than I remembered. Or maybe I was just bigger. There was an adorable garden, though, and even with the low ceilings and crowded rooms, it felt homier than my house. There was a warm and cozy feel to it—maybe it was the roaring fire in the fireplace, the plush, overstuffed furniture, or the smell of freshly baked bread wafting from the kitchen, but I thought maybe it was just Emma herself. She wrapped me in a warm, tight hug when I came through the door and then gave Velma the same treatment—which I could tell made Velma want to vaporize herself. Or maybe Emma.

I swallowed a giggle. Velma did a worse job swallowing hers when Dr. Hunter suggested taking us into his office and showing us some "very exciting documents"—I could tell she knew exactly what I was thinking. Which was something along the lines of *please kill me now.* Or maybe Dr. Hunter.

It was this way when we were kids—I knew Velma well enough that I could almost always tell exactly what she was thinking, and vice versa. It was kind of amazing how after all these years of hating each other, we could slip right back to reading each other's minds.

Fortunately, before we could be trapped in Dr. Hunter's dusty home office for a century of boring history lectures, Emma suggested we sit down to dinner.

I had to admit Velma was right. The centerpiece—an elaborate bouquet of yellow flowers and construction paper swans—was a little over the top. The whole table was kind of Martha Stewart-y, but that didn't seem like a bad thing to me. Especially compared to my mother, who'd never baked a loaf of bread in her entire life, much less woven her own basket to put it in. When I was little, and I told her I wanted to learn how to bake cookies like Aunt Emma did, she made it very clear that was not a satisfactory interest for any daughter of Blake. Just like she always made it very clear, even without saying a word, that I shouldn't care about makeup or fashion. I could have told her that it was misogynistic to dismiss an interest just because it was stereotypically female—and then I could have told her, *Yes, Mom, I know you think I'm an idiot, but I do actually know the word* misogynistic.

But I wouldn't tell her any of that because we weren't exactly on speaking terms anymore. After Marcy vanished, after she suddenly started trying to be all concerned and maternal, I told her I'd spent several years learning not to need my mother, and it turned out I was a better student than she'd thought. After that, she stopped asking me about my feelings. Though she didn't stop staring at me like she wanted to.

Dinner conversation didn't exactly flow, but the roast chicken was delicious. Dr. Hunter droned on about the history of the town. He had some whole theory about what had happened to the original settlers, something to do with sinkholes and "sociopolitical tensions" and mass hysteria, but then even he had to admit he had, like, zero evidence to prove it.

I could have asked why, in that case, he thought he was so superior to the people who thought the town was cursed . . . or the people who thought the settlers had all been kidnapped, or the people who thought they'd gone on a group treasure hunt into the sea caves and never found their way out again, or the people who thought the original Samuel Rogers had murdered them all and then somehow managed to hide the bodies—but I was trying to be polite.

Velma, fortunately, was trying a lot harder than me. She asked a lot of questions about the theory, about the dinner, even about the flowers in the centerpiece, which were called brugmansia and in the same family as the tomato plant . . . and that was already exponentially more than I'd ever wanted to know about a centerpiece.

Aunt Emma wanted to talk about the latest ghost sighting, which she pretty clearly thought was legit. "What?" she said, catching Dr. Hunter's eye roll. "Anything's possible."

"Actually, a wide variety of things are impossible," he corrected her, in a tone that had me wishing I believed in ghosts, because his was not the team I wanted to be on. "This fork, spontaneously lifting out of my hand and into the air? Not possible. To offer one from a veritable plenitude of examples."

"'There are more things in heaven and earth, Horatio, than are dreamt of in your philosophy.'" She said it cheerfully, like she didn't even care her husband was being a jerk. Maybe she was used to it.

"*Hamlet* is fiction," he said. "Like every other ghost story. Especially the ones generated by this town."

"I look forward to you proving that, dear. In the meantime, I'll continue to embrace possibility."

"My wife is determined to believe in the fairy tale this town likes to tell itself," Dr. Hunter told us, and even I had to admit it was obvious that he loved this about her. "Daphne, did you know Emma is the one who first gave your mother the idea for the Crystal Cove game?"

Aunt Emma blushed and tried to shush him, but I wanted to hear more. I knew Emma and my mother had been college roommates, and I knew my mother created her first version of the game right after she graduated. But beyond that, I didn't know much about the birth of my mother's empire, at least not much more than you could learn from Wikipedia.

"She's too humble to brag about it," Dr. Hunter said, "so I'll brag for her. Emma grew up here, of course, and she was always fascinated by the town's founding legend. Apparently when she went to college she was a bit homesick, and the Crystal Cove vanishing is all she could talk about freshman year. Your mother became intrigued, Daphne, and accompanied Emma home that summer, to investigate for herself. The rest is video game history."

"How did I not know this?" I said. "It was all your idea?"

"Without Emma, there would be no *The Curse of Crystal Cove*, no Blake empire," Dr. Hunter said proudly. Emma blushed.

"I hope she gave you a cut of the profits," I joked, then immediately wanted to snatch the words back. Because it was the world's unfunniest joke . . . and because it occurred to me that maybe she should have. I got the sense, from things my mother said, that Emma and the professor weren't exactly rolling in it. It couldn't have felt so great, having a best friend who was a multimillionaire—because of an idea *you* gave her.

But Dr. Hunter and Emma both laughed. "She gave me her friendship," Emma said. "And as you girls surely know, that's reward enough."

On the way out, Velma successfully managed to weasel out of a hug goodbye, slipping through the door before Emma could reach her. But I let her put her arms around me, and I held on tight—and for just a few seconds, I gave in to temptation, and let myself lean on someone else. Someone sturdy and warm.

"You remind me so much of your mother," she said softly as Dr. Hunter scuttled back to his office, leaving us alone.

I couldn't help it—I laughed. "Yeah. Right."

"Razor smart, ambitious, believes she can do anything she sets her mind to? Like mother, like daughter."

"I think my mother'd be surprised to hear that," I said. "She thinks I'm some huge disappointment."

"I can't believe that. The Elizabeth Blake I know would be proud to have a daughter like you. Anyone would."

"Yeah, well, you don't know her that well anymore, do you. She's changed."

"People don't change," Emma said. "Not inside. They may put on different masks, but they're always the same underneath."

I thought about Velma, how she and I seemed to click back together so easily, even after all this time. It was tempting to believe we were still the same kids we used to be before our friendship, and our whole lives, fell apart. But I didn't feel anything like the person I used to be. Sometimes it felt like I'd been wearing a mask so long—the Daphne Blake mask, the pretty, shallow, willing to do anything but cares about nothing mask—I'd forgotten there was an underneath.

"I know this is a difficult time for you," Aunt Emma said. I knew she was talking about Marcy—but for some reason, I didn't resent it the way I usually did. I just nodded. It was difficult. It was impossible. "I'm always here for you, if you need anything."

"I could use another hug," I admitted. And I got one.

I didn't know why Aunt Emma had never had children. But I couldn't help thinking she would have made a good mother.

She would have been the kind of mother who didn't leave.

VELMA

DAPHNE THOUGHT WE SHOULD meet Trey on neutral territory. Those were the words she'd used, "neutral territory," and silly me, I assumed she meant, say, Starbucks.

"How exactly is *this* neutral territory," I said, scanning the scatter of bodies lounging around Fred Jones's pool. Bikini'd flesh roasted in the sun, barrel chests thumped and splashed in the water, and I felt about as inconspicuous as a zombie at a baby shower. Whatever kind of territory this was, it wasn't mine.

Like most schools, Crystal Cove High sorted itself into social groupings, most of them defined by extracurricular club—there were the jocks, the yearbook kids, the student council reps, the gamers (I'd tried that one myself for a bit, but it turned out their unofficial motto was "boys rule, girls drool"), you get the picture.

And then there were the popular kids, who I'd always assumed thought they were too good for after-school activities, but it turned out theirs was just located off campus. According to Daphne, Fred Jones's house was basically an unofficial clubhouse for the golden girls and boys—members only, no losers need apply.

"Fred's Switzerland," she said now. "Free food. A pool. People automatically relax the moment they walk in." Daphne gave me an appraising look. "Except you, that is. You look like you're about to explode."

"Maybe I'm allergic to exclusivity," I said. Wishing I could explode, because then maybe I could stop feeling like there was a high-tension wire running up and down my spine.

"Why do you always have to think like that?" Daphne said. "Not everything's defined by social hierarchy. Did it ever occur to you that maybe people are just people? Who want to hang out with other people?"

"As long as those other people are beautiful and rich and popular?" I tried not to laugh too meanly in her face. "It's only the people at the top of a hierarchy who have the luxury of imagining they can just pretend it away."

"You used to like it over here when we were kids," Daphne pointed out.

I had to admit, that was true. When we were little, back when there was no such thing as popular kids and losers, there was just me and Daphne and Shaggy and Fred, and a summer afternoon at Fred's was like an amusement park and a beach day combined—with better food.

I could admit that, yes. But I didn't have to admit it to her.

"That was a long time ago," I said. "Things change."

Daphne laughed, pointed across the lawn, where Fred was showing off his ability to balance a towering stack of plates on one finger. His limited ability, apparently, because as we watched, they toppled to the ground in a hail of broken ceramic. Fred took a bow, and the small crowd watching him applauded.

"Not everything changes," Daphne said, grinning. "Not Fred."

I allowed myself ten seconds to wonder: What if?

What if change hadn't been inevitable, if Daphne and I had never had our fight. Would this be my life? Would Daphne have yanked me, kicking and screaming, into this life? Or would I have exerted my own gravitational pull, and dragged her down to my level, the two of us, loners together, so never alone?

I couldn't picture it, so I stopped trying. It *was* inevitable, I told myself, as I'd been telling myself for years. That's just what happened with friends like us, two girls with absolutely nothing in common. If we hadn't blown up in a supernova, surely things would have just gradually died away, the energy draining out of us until there was nothing left to keep us together. Maybe that's what happened to every childhood friendship—or every friendship, period, for all I knew. I'd only been on the planet for sixteen years, but that was enough time for me to discern one fundamental law of life: Nothing truly good ever lasted.

We found Trey stuffing his face by the diving board, which was piled high with pizza boxes.

"Can we talk to you for a minute, Trey?" Daphne asked him.

He didn't even bother to look up from his afternoon snack. "You wanna talk about Marcy, right?"

"My, my, what big brains you have," Daphne said, in her best Goldilocks voice.

He looked up at *that*. "Dude, it's not my fault she skipped town, if that's what you're thinking. I don't even know why you're still sulking about it. You ask me, we're all better off."

"You seem pretty sure she ran away," Daphne said. I was impressed by how she managed to keep her voice totally emotionless. It couldn't have been easy, hearing how little Trey cared about his ex.

"Didn't she?" he asked. "That's what the cops told me."

"That's what we're trying to figure out," I said.

His mild confusion—which was pretty much the only expression I'd ever seen on the guy's face—deepened substantially. "Why is *she* talking to me?"

I couldn't get over what Daphne had said before, that Trey was intimidated by me. And I couldn't quite believe it, either. He didn't look intimidated. More like disgusted.

"Maybe not such a big brain after all," Daphne said to me.

"And why are *you* talking to *her*?" Trey asked her.

If Daphne could do it, so could I, I told myself. "I'm talking to you because I don't think Marcy ran away," I told Trey, forcing every last shred of emotion out of my voice. No way would I let him know I cared at all what he thought of me. "And if something else happened to her, I think maybe you had something to do with it. I'm talking to *her* because she thinks the same thing."

Trey flinched. "You're kidding me." His laughter sounded pretty forced, and a tiny bit frightened. "Detective Dinkley's on the case?"

That nickname.

I hated that nickname with every fiber of my being.

I could feel Daphne watching me, waiting for me to freak out. Probably feeling guilty since, after all, she was the one who'd invented it.

And basically ruined a year of my life.

I did not freak out.

"Yes," I told Trey, and I made myself smile. "Detective Dinkley is on the case. And she's determined there's only one person with motive, opportunity, and a poorly hidden grudge against his ex-girlfriend." We'd all been talking a little quietly, but now I raised my voice to an almost yell, to make sure I'd be overheard. "You said we're all better off without Marcy—did you do something to make sure we'd be without her?"

The blood drained out of Trey's face. "Could you, like, stop yelling?"

He ushered us, quickly, into the pool house—which was already occupied by a homecoming princess and her thick-muscled (and thick-headed) boyfriend, knotted together. I could feel my face burning, but Daphne just coughed, loudly, then said, *"Out."*

They leapt up and scurried away, almost apologetically, like they couldn't believe they'd almost managed to cross the great and powerful Daphne Blake. She seemed so sure people were intimidated by me—I wondered if she realized they were intimidated by her, too.

Once we were safely alone behind closed doors, Trey dropped onto a lounge chair and got serious. "Okay. What do you want to know."

Daphne turned to me, like she was waiting to follow my lead. So I led. "Let's start with opportunity. Walk us through where you were Friday night through Saturday morning,"

I said. Daphne and I agreed that if something had happened to Marcy, that was the most likely window of time. After the party, and before she was supposed to meet Daphne at the coffee shop. Whatever happened in those dark hours between, *that* was our mystery.

"You're joking, right?" Trey said.

"I thought word on the street was that I had no sense of humor."

Daphne snorted.

"Dude, I was at Shaggy's party all night," Trey said. "Which you know, because you were there. In your turtleneck." He snickered, then turned to Daphne as if he was waiting for her to join in. She gave him a stone face. "Yeah. Okay. Whatever. I was at Shaggy's. Then I crashed. Woke up around noon to his freaking dog licking my face."

"I always thought Scooby had better taste," Daphne murmured.

"What'd you say?" Trey asked.

She smiled at him, suddenly all sugar and spice. "Nothing."

Trey scowled. "Ask anyone. There were like fifteen people crashing at the house. Everyone saw me. So there you go, there's my, whatever, alibi thingy. We done here?" He started to stand up.

"No," I snapped. *"Sit."*

He sat. Obedient as a dog. Intimidated.

Daphne caught my eye, smirked: *Told you so.*

"You dated for how long?" I said, brisk and efficient. Maybe being Detective Dinkley wasn't so bad.

"Six months. Then she dumped me."

So now we'd moved on to motive.

"And why did she dump you? Other than the obvious reasons."

He looked like he wanted to argue, or at least insult me back, but . . . he didn't. "She wouldn't say. But you ask me, I think she was hooking up with someone else."

"What makes you say that?" Daphne put in.

"Uh . . ." He blushed.

"Come on," Daphne urged him. "If you ever cared about Marcy, just help us out here."

He didn't answer, and I wondered if he even had the capacity to care. He at least seemed to have the capacity to feel embarrassed, judging by the fire in his cheeks. I decided to give bad cop a try. Or at least, frank cop. "Trey, let's be clear. You are not important to us—or to this situation. So whatever it is you're trying not to say, just say it. No one's going to judge you. Mostly because there is literally no one in this room who cares about you or what you do, whatsoever. We're here about Marcy. So spit it out."

And, miraculously, he spat it out.

"I was jealous, okay? She was being all squirrelly, getting texts in the middle of the night, lying about where she was, and, like, no one in their right mind would cheat on *me* . . . but just in case, I started following her."

"Stalker," Daphne said. Not helpful—and I gave her a stern look to remind her of this. We needed him to spill his guts.

"I caught her going down to the beach one day, like, before dawn. Which doesn't make sense because the only thing Marcy hated more than early morning was the beach. Except . . ."

"Except?" I said.

"Except if she was meeting someone, I guess. That's when I saw her with him."

"Who?"

He shook his head. "No idea. I was too far away. Just saw her hugging this dude in an orange wet suit, and I got out of there. You want to know what's going on with Marcy? You should talk to that loser—I bet you he knows."

"Thank you, Trey," Daphne said, and managed to make it sound like she meant it.

"I don't get why you're even bothering," he said in a sulky voice.

"Because she's my best friend, Trey. That means something to me."

Trey stood up. He was several inches taller than both of us, and suddenly, towering over us, made me feel very small. "You think you know her so well, D? I thought so, too. I thought she loved me, so I guess that makes me the idiot for missing the obvious. But maybe you should think about what you're missing. Sounds to me like she was lying to both of us."

I waited for Daphne to spit something back in his face, but she just walked out of the pool house without saying anything. So I followed.

"He's right, you know," I said quietly, once we were safely out of Trey's earshot. "He is an idiot."

She looked like she wanted to argue, but all she said was, "Thanks."

* * *

That night, Jerry Printz, the manager at the Haunted Village, called, right in the middle of dinner. I assumed he wanted to talk to my mother, but he was actually calling for me, to tell me not to bother coming in for my shift the next morning.

"They're shutting down for a few days," I explained when I sat back down at the table. "Safety investigation, supposedly. But you know he's just putting on a show to reassure people." It was one thing to call yourself a haunted village—it was another thing altogether to let people start believing you were haunted by an angry ghost.

"I'm not surprised," my mother said. "They need the anniversary festival to go off without a hitch. It's not just a big part of the bottom line, it *is* the bottom line."

"I hope it's full of hitches," I said. "With what they're

doing to you? That place deserves to go under." Not to mention what they'd done to our whole family. The Haunted Village stole our home—sometimes I felt like it stole the lives we were supposed to have—and I was ready to dance at its funeral.

"Don't say that, mi amor," my mother said. "It's not just the Village that's at stake here. It's the town. Why do you think it's a tourist trap instead of, say, a golf course?"

I sighed. The last thing I needed was one of my mother's patented lectures on Crystal Cove zoning laws. I had them all memorized. "Because the town attaches restrictions to all new properties, making sure that every new development stays in keeping with the character of the town," I said dutifully, hoping to head her off before she really got started.

"That's right. But there are plenty of people in Crystal Cove—and especially outside of Crystal Cove—who'd like to see those rules go away. If businesses here start losing money, going under? Those voices get louder and louder. All it takes is one executive action by the town council to turn us into a development free-for-all. And suddenly we're all living in some billionaire's front yard."

"I know, Mom. I get it. I got it the last twenty times you said it. And I've signed every single one of your petitions."

"Your mother's passionate," my father said. "It's why we love her."

It was the first thing he'd said the entire meal, and he

looked like saying it had drained him of energy. It wasn't his fault; I knew that. I even knew it wasn't the Haunted Village's fault, either. His depression stuff might have started when we lost our home, but I knew the difference between a catalyst and an underlying problem. I knew plenty, because I'd done years of research, trying to find something to fill the cold, empty space at the heart of our family. There wasn't some obvious, single reason, just like there wasn't any easy shortcut to a happy ending. There was, as my mother always said, just treatment and love and time. And sometimes all those things worked, and things were better for a while. Sometimes things were worse, and when they were, it was hard not to look for someone to blame.

I wondered if that was why my mother was so passionate about protecting Crystal Cove from evil real estate developers—if hating them was her way of loving my dad, of blaming someone who wasn't him. I wished I could find something to pour myself into like that, a way to fool myself into thinking I was helping my father. Instead of just secretly wishing he would become someone else.

I loved him. Of course I loved him. But I also wished he was more like the man he used to be. And occasionally—though I would never have admitted it out loud to anyone—I wished he was more like Dr. Hunter. The professor was so excited about the world, about its possibilities. It felt like he was always in motion, even when he was sitting still, because his brain never stopped moving. And just being around him made my brain feel more alive, more engaged, more awake. I hated myself for comparing the two of them.

But I couldn't help it.

* * *

The bad news about my canceled morning shift was that I wouldn't get paid. The good news was that it meant Daphne and I could spend our morning on a stakeout. We parked Daphne's car in the parking lot by the surfers' cove, as close as we could get to the beach without risking that someone might spot us peeping out the windows. From the passenger-side window, we could see most of the long sandy stretch of beach, all the way to the sea caves that bordered its northern edge. There were only a handful of surfers out that morning, all of them in wet suits, none of them bright orange.

Daphne gulped her jumbo coffee. "Imagine loving someone so much you were willing to get up at dawn for them."

"You're doing that right now, for Marcy."

"Fair point," Daphne said. "So what are you doing here?"

Before I had to come up with an answer, a rap on the window startled us both. Emma Hunter's face peered in through the glass.

"What do we do?" I said, panicked.

"Roll down the window?" Daphne suggested, and did just that.

Emma smiled warmly. But then, she did everything

warmly. It was her brand. "I thought that was your car, Daphne."

I wasn't sure what I was more worried about: Emma busting our stakeout or forcing us out of the car so we could hug. It's not that I had anything against Emma Hunter, I just barely knew her. So I didn't exactly love that every time she saw me she acted like she was some kind of loving relative who wanted to smother me with affection and hugs. I hate it when people who barely know you pretend they do. And I especially hate when that pretense comes with a hug.

"What are you girls doing out here so early?"

"Oh, we, uh . . ." My mind was a black hole.

"School project," Daphne said brightly.

Emma looked dubious. "What kind of school project has you out on the beach at dawn?"

Daphne didn't even hesitate. "It's an earth science thing. Totally lame, I know. And trust me, I tried to get Velma to do all the work, because she has all the brains, but she has this insane idea that a group project means everyone in the group should participate. Can you imagine?"

Emma laughed, shook her head, and I realized she was distracted enough by Daphne's charm that she wasn't going to think too much about the details. Clearly I didn't have *all* the brains. Daphne was a genius.

"What are *you* doing here, Emma?" she asked.

Emma waved toward the sea caves. "The tide pools have

such lush life, I like to come out here at dawn sometimes and take photos. I suppose I'm a bit of an amateur photographer. Silly hobby, I suppose, but it's mine."

"Not silly!" Daphne chirped. "It sounds awesome."

"I'd be happy to take you girls on a personal tour someday."

"That sounds, uh . . ." I shuddered, imagining myself setting foot in one of those caves. No one actually knew how far the network of caves stretched underground and into the sea, but it was supposedly miles and miles, all of it pitch-black. It was a fact that some of the people who wandered into those caves never came back—there were even some who believed the sea caves were the answer to what happened to the original settlers, although Professor Hunter said he'd found no evidence for that theory. Either way, I was not volunteering to go inside.

"I would love that, Emma!" Daphne said, then hopped out of the car just long enough to give her a hug and send her on her way.

Once we were alone again, I asked her if she'd lost her mind. "You want to take a tour of those caves?"

"Are you kidding?" Daphne asked. "I just didn't want her to spend too much time thinking about what we might be doing here. Now she's on her way home thinking about some ridiculously boring tour of the tide pools. Problem solved. Trust me, I'm never actually going into those caves again. Remember our field trip?"

Oh, I remembered. Third grade, class trip, wrong turn, dead flashlight, wandering in the dark for maybe five minutes, but it felt like a hundred years.

"It was the only time I ever saw Marcy really afraid," Daphne added. Her voice wobbled.

I wanted to tell her not to worry, that we would find Marcy safe and sound, that everything would be okay. I wanted to *make* everything okay for her. But I couldn't do the latter, so it didn't seem right to promise the former. Instead, I just sat there, trying to figure out whether I should pretend not to notice her fear, or find a way to soothe it. Before I had to decide, I caught a flash of orange in the corner of my eye.

"Look!" I cried. Daphne was already pressed to the window. She'd seen it, too. A guy at the far edge of the beach, his back to us, his hair the same color as the sand, his wet suit the color of a traffic cone. *Turn around*, I willed him. *Show us your face.*

He didn't turn around. He whistled, and a dog bounded toward him. A dog I recognized.

"No way," Daphne said as the guy turned to greet his dog. The two of them headed toward the parking lot, getting close enough that we could see the guy's face. We could even see the bone-shaped biscuits he was tossing in the dog's mouth.

"No. Freaking. Way," Daphne said. "Not possible."

Sherlock Holmes said that once you eliminate the impossible, whatever was left has to be the truth, no matter how improbable. It was definitely improbable, but it was also here, in front of us, in the flesh, the truth about Marcy's secret boyfriend: Shaggy Rogers.

DAPHNE

"NO WAY." I GAPED at Shaggy across the table. We'd taken him to Giuseppi's Slice of Heaven, because when you wanted something from Shaggy, the best way to get it was bribing him with food. The guy couldn't resist a free pizza. We'd bought him two. "No. Way."

"Why does she keep saying that?" Shaggy asked Velma. "Is there, like, something wrong with her?"

You could say that. My fuses were blown. My mental capacity had winnowed down to two words: No. Way. *No. Way.*

No way Marcy's secret boyfriend was, of all people, *Shaggy* Rogers.

Marcy thought Shaggy was a joke. *I* was the one always telling her he was a good guy. Telling her, *He's more interesting than you think! He's smarter than you realize!* And then

Marcy would point out that I hadn't had a real conversation with him since we were ten years old, so what did I know . . . and she was right. Good for parties, Marcy always said. Otherwise? A total dud. And his dog smelled.

Add to that the fact that he was 100 percent not in any way her type. She went for pretty and dumb (Exhibit #1: Trey Moloney). She liked to boss them around, she told me, and encouraged me to try the same. It wasn't my thing. But for the entire time I'd known Marcy, even back when the only boys we cared about were the famous ones whose pictures we hung on our bedroom walls, it was hers.

"You and Marcy?" I said. "No way. I just don't believe it."

"Like, what's she talking about?" Shaggy said, his mouth full of pizza. Add it to the list of reasons Marcy would never have cheated on Trey with *him*. She was a fiend about chewing with your mouth shut. She wouldn't even let me chew gum.

"She's talking about you and Marcy Heller," Velma said, fortunately clueing in that she was going to have to take the lead on this one. "Was she cheating on Trey with you?"

"Like . . . whoa." Shaggy dropped his slice of pizza—the dog, who he'd somehow smuggled into the restaurant, gobbled it up in a millisecond. "Whoa. Chill. Who, uh, who's saying that? Uh, yeah, like she said, no way. *No way.*"

"Methinks he protests a bit too much," Velma said. "And more than a bit unconvincingly."

"Look, I don't know what you heard, but Marcy and I were *not* together, not like that," Shaggy said. It sounded true.

Velma looked like she'd heard something else, though, underneath his words. "But you wanted to be," she said softly. "You care about her."

"Yeah, of course I care about her," he said. "Why else would I—"

His mouth snapped shut like a steel trap. Not even the pizza was getting through that. He knew something, something that mattered. And no way was I walking out of there without finding out. I informed him of this. Then I told him that if he expected me to believe he cared about Marcy even a tiny bit, he would tell me what he knew, because this wasn't exactly a time for secrets. Because she was in trouble.

He sighed. "Yeah. I know."

"You don't think she ran away?" Velma asked.

Shaggy shook his head.

"Did you happen to mention that to your mom?" I said, in, okay, a not particularly friendly voice. "Because she's not exactly winning my vote for cop of the year so far."

"I . . . I can't tell her that. Not without telling, like, some other stuff that, like, I'm not supposed to tell her."

"What—"

"Or you!" he cut in. "Or, like, any living soul. I took, like, a sacred, solemn oath."

I was about to light him on fire with my superpowered rage glare—or at least, I was definitely going to fantasize, in painful detail, about doing so. But Velma apparently had a different strategy in mind.

Kindness. Go figure.

"It must be hard for you, feeling like you know something that could help, but you're sworn to secrecy," she said sympathetically.

"It's, like, torture," Shaggy agreed.

"Shaggy, whatever secrets you promised to keep for Marcy, those secrets could be the key to finding her," Velma said softly. "Helping her. It's not a betrayal to tell us what you know. I swear. We're not the cops. We're not her parents. We're just—well, Daphne is, at least, um—"

"We're her friends," I said, and figured it was sort of, technically true, since Velma was my friend and I was Marcy's friend. There must have been some kind of math rule to cover that equation. "I love her, Shaggy," I went on. "I just want what's best for her. I want to *find* her. If you know anything . . ." It was so strange, sitting here with these two people I barely knew anymore, feeling like they were the only two people on the planet I could count on. *"Please."*

Scooby barked. "See, even Scoob wants you to."

Shaggy ruffled his dog's fur, and for a second, it was like he was really considering that thought, that Scooby was encouraging him to trust us. I didn't care if he got his advice from a Great Dane. He could get it from a cockroach, for all I cared, as long as it pointed him in our direction.

"Okay," he said. "You want the story?"

"Yes!" Velma and I shouted in unison.

"Like, I get it," he said. "I'll tell you." He rubbed his forehead. He rubbed his chin. He rubbed his dog. We waited.

I appreciated it, I did. I wouldn't have expected Shaggy to care this much about keeping anyone's secrets—or about anything period. It was obviously killing him to break Marcy's confidence. The hesitation made me like him more. It also made me want to strangle him. We were wasting time.

"It was a few months ago," Shaggy said finally. "She'd had some huge blowup with her parents. They were supposed to come visit and they flaked on her or something?"

I remembered—Marcy had been waiting for that visit for months. Not that she would ever have admitted it out loud, but I knew she was dying to see her parents again. Then, at the last minute, they postponed. Indefinitely.

Who asks their kid for a rain check?

Marcy pretended like she didn't care, and usually I would have ignored her, made her come spend the weekend at my place, cheered her with greasy pizza and homemade face masks—but that was the rare weekend I was forced to go stay at my mother's place in the city. So I'd had to leave her alone.

According to Shaggy, she'd gone out for a walk, late at

night—"Just to think," Shaggy said. But I knew Marcy; I knew that kind of walk. She was out looking for trouble. And she'd found it. Trouble in the shape of a vintage sports car in pristine condition, parked on a curb with the keys in the ignition. Like the universe was offering it to her as a compensation prize. She took it.

The prize.

The *car.*

Shaggy told us that she drove it around for hours, speeding faster and faster in loops around the outskirts of town. I could picture it, so easily. Marcy's hair streaming in the wind, face turned recklessly to the sky, foot slamming the gas, urging the car faster and faster, and even though it was months ago, I felt myself tensing up for her, for the disaster on the horizon, for the way she acted like she didn't care about her own life. Maybe because she wasn't convinced anyone else did, either. *I care*, I thought, wishing I could beam it to her past self, to her present one, wherever she was. *Believe me. I care.*

"She got lucky," Shaggy said. "She was back in town, only going like twenty miles an hour when it happened."

When some kind of animal—a coyote, maybe?—ran into the road. When she spun the wheel to save its life, veered off the road, into a tree. Totaled the stolen car. Panicked, tried to flee the scene, got scooped up by a patrol car, spent the night in jail. "That's why I know about it," Shaggy said. "My mom was out of town and needed me to grab something for her from the office."

"In the middle of the night?" Velma asked.

"I could've done it the next morning, but I got bored. I don't sleep much."

There was something about the way he said it . . . something kind of sad, almost wistful. Shaggy Rogers was more of a mystery than I'd ever expected. But he wasn't the mystery we needed to solve, not today.

"It's not like we were friends or anything, but she was freaking out, and she didn't have anyone, so I guess . . ." He shrugged. "Anyway, after that night, we were, like, friends. We had a secret—that'll do it, sometimes."

"So why don't *I* know about all this?" I asked him. I was supposed to be the keeper of Marcy's secrets. I was the "anyone" she apparently thought she didn't have. "If Marcy stole a car, ended up in jail, wouldn't I know? Wouldn't everyone?"

"That's the thing, the old dude made it all go away. Except for the cop on duty, I was the only person who knew, so I was the only person she could talk to about it, I guess."

I tried not to let it hurt. "What old dude?"

Shaggy said he only knew what Marcy had told him. That some time after Shaggy left but before sunrise, the owner of the car, an "old dude" of unspecified oldness, had shown up and made a deal with Marcy. If she agreed to work some odd jobs for him, and keep it a total secret, he would make the charges disappear. Permanently. Her other option: reform school, maybe jail. Her choice.

It was one thing, getting into trouble in hopes your parents would bother to remember you existed, maybe even come home. It was another thing to get into the kind of trouble that would yank you out of your home. Send you away. Especially if it happened the night your parents proved they didn't care about you at all. That they were never moving home, no matter what kind of trouble you got into. That you were on your own.

"You don't know his name?" I asked.

Shaggy shook his head.

"Or anything else about him?" Velma pressed.

"All I know is that it was okay for a while, but then Marcy started to flip out. Whatever he was making her do, she didn't want to do it. He was, like, blackmailing her, holding the jail thing over her head. She knew if she stopped doing what he wanted, he'd just call the cops."

"That night she got trapped in the Haunted Village jail," Velma said suddenly. "What if Marcy had started pushing back—what if this guy was sending her a message somehow? Reminding her what was at stake."

"Yeah," Shaggy said. "The guy, he was the reason she was there in the first place. He made sure she could get inside. It wasn't your mom, V. Marcy felt really bad about that, if it helps."

Velma made a noise that made it pretty clear it did not help.

"It makes sense," I said. The puzzle pieces were starting to make a picture. "We know Marcy was done. That's what she meant after your party, when she said she was going to fix things, make things right—what if she told this guy she wasn't going to do whatever he wanted anymore. And what if he . . ." I swallowed. *What if.*

"This is good news," Velma said. "This guy, whoever he is, could be the key."

"Yeah, whoever he is," I said. "But how are we supposed to figure that one out?"

Shaggy cleared his throat. "Uh, this may be, like, a terrible idea, but . . . I think maybe I can help with that."

VELMA

"YOU'RE ABSOLUTELY SURE THIS is okay?" I asked Shaggy.

"It's okay," Daphne said. "Just like it was okay the hundred other times you asked."

"I mean, are you defining *okay* as in 'totally legal and we'd get, like, a gold star for doing it'?" Shaggy asked. He stopped at the top of the steps, just before we got to the door of the police station. "Or, *okay* as in 'probably we won't get caught'?"

"I was kind of hoping for option A," I admitted.

"In that case . . ."

"Not to resort to cliché, but they say you can't make an omelet without breaking some eggs," Daphne said, pretty obviously dying to go inside. "Which is a cliché for a reason. That reason being it's true."

"I don't mind breaking eggs," I told her. "I'm just not so sure about breaking my permanent record. Or the law, for that matter."

"We're not breaking anything," Shaggy said quickly. "Just, like . . . bending. A little."

"Look, you don't have to come in with us if you don't want to," Daphne said, but the way she was looking at me . . . it reminded me of how she used to look when she begged me to come with her to her ballet lessons, or to ice cream with her arguing parents, or to visit her second cousin in San Francisco. *Please, pretty please with a Dinkley on top*, she would say, which made just little enough sense to make me laugh, and then I would always give in to whatever she wanted. Because back then I loved her, and I loved making her happy.

"We're in this together," I said, and together, we opened the door and went inside.

At this time of night, in this small of a town, there was only one guy in the front room, a young, uniformed officer with a blond mustache. His gaze was fixed on his computer.

"Hey, Manny," Shaggy said, doing a good job of acting like a guy without a care in the world. In other words, acting exactly the way he always acted. I was starting to wonder how much of the Shaggy I knew was just for show. But why go to the trouble? "I'm just running in to grab my mom's umbrella. She thinks she forgot it at the office again. Okay?"

"No problem," the cop said, without ever turning away

from the screen. He waved Shaggy by, without looking up long enough to notice the two girls and one dog who were following him.

"What happens tomorrow," I whispered to Shaggy, "when he asks your mother about her umbrella?"

Shaggy let us into his mother's office, which was unlocked. That made me feel an inch better—if there was no lock on the door, wasn't that almost an invitation to go inside?

"Chill. Manny only works nights, and my mom only works days, so, like, *never* gonna happen. And even if it did? Manny's so addicted to his gaming, he already, like, forgot we were here." He flipped on the computer and typed in a password: *1 2 3 4*. "As you can see, my cop mom is über-serious about security."

"What now?" Daphne asked.

Shaggy's fingers were already flying across the keyboard. It was weird how natural he looked at a computer—I would have taken him for one of those guys who only ever went online when he needed to order dinner. "Now we pull up Marcy's file, snag the name of the dude who owned the car she wrecked, and we'll have a prime suspect. Easy as pie." His stomach grumbled, like even under these circumstances, his body couldn't ignore the invocation of food.

"Have you done this before?" I asked. He seemed way too confident for this to be his first time.

"No way!" The way he said it—as if I'd accused him of

robbing a bank—suggested this whole thing might be slightly a bigger deal than he'd let on. "I just pay attention. You never know what you might need to know . . . you know?"

I knew. I was just surprised Shaggy did, since he never seemed to be paying much attention to anything. I was even more surprised he was taking this kind of risk for us—for Marcy, specifically. He must really care about her.

I believed him that there was nothing romantic between them. But I paid attention, too, and I was pretty sure he wished there were. It was the wistfulness in his voice when he talked about her. It was the doggedness with which he'd tried not to betray her confidence. It was the look on his face when we told him we'd found evidence suggesting Marcy hadn't run away. Even though he already suspected it himself. Having a theory was one thing, proving it was another. He cared too much to want to be right.

I wondered if Marcy knew how much. I wondered if she cared for him, too. If she'd daydreamed what it would be like, his arms around her, his lips pressed to hers. It was almost as impossible to imagine Marcy wanting to date Shaggy as it was to imagine . . . well, wanting to date Shaggy. But then, I had a hard time imagining wanting to date anyone in this town.

It's not that I didn't think about it—having a boyfriend, going to school dances, making out in the woods, or whatever it is teenagers were supposed to do when they thought they were in love. But it's not like there were any viable candidates to choose from. And it's not like anyone in Crystal Cove would ever think of *me* like that, whether I wanted it or not, so what was even the point of wanting?

"Weird," Shaggy murmured.

Daphne and I peered over his shoulder at the database he'd hacked.

"What?" I asked.

Shaggy pointed to Marcy's name on the screen, paired with the date and time of the accident. "Someone created a file," he said. "Once you make an entry for someone, it stays in the system forever—but the file itself is empty."

"Like someone went and erased it," Daphne said.

Someone who didn't want any record of their connection with Marcy Heller. We'd run smack into a brick wall—but I could feel it, all the answers waiting for us on the other side. "Any ideas?" I said.

Daphne shrugged, but I caught it, the glint in her eyes. She had an idea, all right—something she didn't want to say in front of Shaggy, maybe, so I let it go.

We left the station together, and he apologized for not being more help. We told him that he'd been more help than anyone, and then we gave him a hug, each of us. It seemed like he needed it.

"Okay, out with it," I told Daphne, the moment we were alone in her car.

"What?"

"Whatever it is you didn't want to say in front of Shaggy," I said.

"How did you know?"

"Apparently, I know you," I said. "So?"

"It's possible I have an idea," she allowed. "But I have a feeling you're not going to like it."

"How do you know?"

She grinned and swung the car in an abrupt U-turn. "Because I know you, too."

* * *

"I don't like this," I said as we entered the offices of the *Crystal Cove Howler.*

Daphne looked smug. "I do so love being right."

As far as I was concerned, the *Howler* was a stain on Crystal Cove, something that should have been washed away a long time ago. That's what my mother always said about it, and as usual, she made a good case. No matter what happened, the tabloid found a way to ratchet it up into a ridiculous scandal or horror story—and it was very good at that, which meant most of what the outside world knew about Crystal Cove came from the *Howler.* And the people who lived here were just as enthralled by it—the only reason people believed Marcy's stupid ghost story was because they read it in print. If it was in the newspaper—even a fake, full-of-lies-and-ridiculous-fairy-tales newspaper like the *Howler*—it must be true.

I liked facts, and I also liked stories—what I hated was for the two of them to get all mixed up. That was the reason I liked playing detective so much, actually. Solving a mystery was the process of sorting through a bunch of different possible stories and sifting out the facts so you could piece together something true. The *Howler* didn't care about true; it only cared about exciting. So I had no clue why Daphne thought coming here would help us get any closer to the true story of what happened to Marcy. "You have to take help where you can find it," she said. And it's not like I had any better ideas. So here we were.

We introduced ourselves to the receptionist and told her we wanted to speak to Milford Jones, the owner and editor in chief. "We have a hot tip about the hauntings," Daphne said, and apparently that was exactly the right thing to say, because a minute later, we were in Milford Jones's office. He shook our hands and beamed a used-car-salesman smile.

"Always pleased to meet loyal readers," he said. "You girls at the high school with my Freddie?"

"That's right, Mr. Jones," Daphne said. "We've known Fred since we were all in diapers."

It was hard to believe that a lying slimeball like Milford Jones was Fred's uncle, but his face was the proof: They looked just like each other, right down to the swoop of blond bangs and the game-show-host teeth.

We introduced ourselves, and his eyes widened when he

heard Daphne's last name. "Yes," she said, sounding weary, like this was a conversation she was already tired of having. "*That* Blake."

"We've published many a profile on your mother, but unfortunately she's never had time to sit down for an interview." He was practically drooling.

"She's very busy," Daphne said, smiling sweetly. She could be polite when she had to be. Or at least when she wanted to be, which didn't exactly amount to the same thing. I wondered whether she'd actually read any of the Elizabeth Blake profiles published in the *Howler*. Probably not, or she definitely wouldn't have been able to pull off that smile—hatchet jobs on Elizabeth Blake seemed to be an annual tradition at the *Howler*. Every year Milford Jones came up with another conspiracy theory about how she and her gaming empire were going to destroy the town. Weirdly, every year, the town kept not getting destroyed.

"If you're in a position to put in a good word for me and the work we do here, I'd be much obliged," he told Daphne.

"I definitely plan to tell her how helpful you've been today," Daphne said, as if he'd already done exactly what we wanted.

Jones got the message, loud and clear. "All right, then—how can I help you?"

"The better question is, how can we help you?" Daphne said. "We've got a lead for you."

"Hmm." He looked skeptical, but sat back in his chair, gestured for us to go ahead, do our best.

That was why Daphne wanted to come here, she'd said in the car. Of course he was skeptical. Who wouldn't be? Who would actually listen to two teenage girls with a conspiracy theory and some information—or at least, evidence of a lack of information—they'd basically stolen from the police? Who else but the man whose job it was to take everything seriously, no matter how ridiculous? The man with a vested interest in this particular story, because his tabloid was churning out new articles about the Crystal Cove ghost nearly every hour. The man who'd made Marcy a star. *He wants to believe something nefarious is going on*, Daphne had argued. Teen runaways weren't exciting—they were depressing. *We'll give him an exciting story*, Daphne said. *And then we'll put him to work.*

"It's about Marcy Heller," Daphne said, and his eyes lit up.

"You've come to the right place!" he said brightly. "Terrible, that one. Just awful."

"You seem pretty cheerful about something so awful," I pointed out.

He shrugged. "Well, you know what they say in the news biz. Bad news is great news!"

I glanced at Daphne, a little worried. The idea of Marcy's disappearance as good news might turn her into a volcano and spatter him with the molten lava of her rage. I was also wondering if it had just occurred to her, as it had occurred to me, that Milford Jones had a lot to gain from the dramatic and mysterious events of the last several days. I wondered how many more people were reading the *Howler* now that they thought the town might really have its very own angry ghost.

But Daphne was laser-focused on the task at hand. She told Milford Jones everything we'd learned about Marcy's car accident, the possibility of blackmail, the missing police report—and that's when we got him. He leaned forward, hungry.

"You're telling me someone *erased* the report? Someone involved in the disappearance of an innocent young girl?"

"And probably involved in these so-called ghost sightings," I said.

"And, let me guess, you want me to use my rather considerable resources to dig into this, see if I can come up with anything?"

"If there was a car accident, there's got to be evidence of it," I told him. "Tow trucks, 911 calls, car mechanic records, eyewitnesses—*someone* arrested her, right? That someone knows what was in that report. That's a lot of possible 'anything.'"

"So why don't you track that down yourself?" he asked.

"We're trying," Daphne admitted. "But it's not exactly

easy to get people to listen to us. So we have to use every means at our disposal."

"And you're assuming *I'm* at your disposal?"

"We are." Daphne said it like he had already agreed, and it was almost like he believed her. I made a mental note to get her to teach me how that worked—how you could make someone do anything, and somehow make them believe it was their idea.

"Okay. I'm intrigued," Milford Jones allowed. "I'll look into it. And what will you be doing for me in return?"

It hadn't even occurred to me we should have an answer ready for that one . . . but of course, Daphne had it on the tip of her tongue.

"An exclusive," Daphne said. "Once we solve the case, you'll get the exclusive interview about how we did it."

"Teen detectives solve the Case of the Vanishing Girl?" He closed his eyes like he was trying to visualize the headline. "Yeah, I can sell that."

So it was a deal. I gave him my cell number, and he promised to call the moment he found anything useful for us.

"Oh, one more thing," Daphne said as we were on our way out, and something about the extremely casual way she said it made me realize this was the most important thing of all. "You might want to look into George Baker. See if there's any record of him owning a vintage car. Or any connection to Marcy Heller at all."

"George Baker as in the George Baker married to your mother?" Milford said, eyebrows sky-high. "Care to elaborate on why I should do that?"

"Nope." Daphne flounced out of the office and, much less flouncy, I followed her.

"*Now* do you care to elaborate?" I asked her, once we were back in the parking lot. "And before you say no, can I remind you we're a team?"

She sighed. "Think about it. The pieces all fit together—the real estate printouts, the supposed ghost sightings, the 'older dude.' And that weekend Marcy stole the car? I was at my mom's place in the city. You know who *wasn't*? Her husband. Out of town. On 'business.' Does that not seem seriously suspicious to you?"

"I guess it's . . . possible?"

"Like you have a better idea?" Daphne snapped.

"Well . . ." I tilted my head in the direction we'd come. "Has it occurred to you that the *Howler* probably has a lot of new readers this week?"

"You think *Fred's uncle* kidnapped Marcy and faked a bunch of ghost sightings just to, what? Improve his *sales numbers*?"

"It makes as much sense as your stepfather suddenly deciding to turn from a lawyer into a criminal."

"Why are you so against my theory?" Daphne retorted. "Do you think it's just inevitably wrong, because it's *mine*? Am I too dumb to figure this out myself, is that it?"

"That's not it!"

"Then what?"

Tread carefully, I thought, and considered not treading at all.

"Do you, uh, think maybe you're just looking for a reason to hate him?" I asked quietly.

"Do you think I need more reasons?" she asked icily. "And you should be the first person to suspect him! You know better than anyone how ruthless he can be, how he doesn't care who gets hurt."

She was right, in a way. George Baker had hurt a lot of people—after he negotiated the deal to sell the town museum, he'd negotiated a lot more deals on behalf of his clients. He'd probably had his fingers in half the town's real estate deals over the last few years. Buying up Crystal Cove land was his specialty—as was representing secret clients. According to my mother, there were acres and acres of land in town owned by shadow corporations. No one even knew who they were . . . except George Baker.

"Okay, it's definitely possible," I said. "But what do you want to do about it? Confront him?"

"Not yet. We need evidence. He and my mother are going out tomorrow for 'date night,' vomit. I'm babysitting. And as soon as the girls go to bed, I'm investigating. You should come, too."

"Me? Really?"

"Why are you always so surprised that I want you to come along? I thought we were in this together. I thought we were a team."

I hadn't really thought about it, but once I did, I didn't need to think too hard. Of course I was surprised. Because I'd made a mistake before, assuming we were a team, assuming Daphne wanted me at her side wherever she went—and I'd suffered the consequences of that assumption. She could call us a team all she wanted, but part of me was still waiting for the other shoe to drop. Not that I was going to say any of that out loud.

Maybe I didn't have to.

Daphne shrugged. "Yeah. I guess if I were you, I wouldn't trust me, either."

We drove home in silence.

* * *

Daphne's house was bigger than I remembered. (And I remembered it plenty big.) It was also colder. When we were kids, it always felt like such a warm and welcoming place to go, a place that had everything we didn't—the toys my parents said we couldn't afford, the snacks my parents said were too unhealthy to eat, the cable channels and streaming services and gaming system my parents said were a waste of time. Bedtime was an hour later at Daphne's house, and even after we turned the lights out, sleeping over at Daphne's meant lying side by side on her plush rug, staring up at the glow-in-the-dark stars on her ceiling, whispering feverishly until, sometime after midnight and before dawn, we finally fell asleep. I couldn't remember most of the secrets we'd shared on those nights, but I remembered the *feeling* of them, like they were the most important things in the world. Every time Daphne trusted me with one, it was like getting a handful of gold.

Maybe the house felt cold now because I knew too much about the family living here—Daphne not speaking to her mother or stepfather, the little sisters who hopefully hadn't noticed how much their big sister despised them.

After she let me in, Daphne eased the door shut behind me and we tiptoed up the stairs. "I put the girls to bed an hour early," she whispered. "And they just . . . went. Can you believe it? They're so well behaved."

I couldn't tell whether she was disgusted or impressed. Maybe a little bit of both. I followed her down a dark hallway and into her father's office. It looked exactly like I remembered it, stuffed with books and file cabinets and framed photos of Daphne. Cluttered and cozy, except for the desk, which was almost empty—two stacks of papers, neatly piled, a pencil holder, a stapler, all of it lined up so perfectly it was like someone had used a ruler. "My stepfather's using the desk temporarily," Daphne said.

The idea that George Baker could be involved in something

like this was still hard to wrap my head around. I whispered, not wanting to wake the girls. "You really think—"

"You can talk like a normal person," Daphne cut in. "My dad had the door soundproofed. I think he and my mom would come in here to yell at each other, back when they were still—you know, in a yelling place." She was already rifling through the piles on the desk and looking in all the drawers.

I was getting a bad feeling about this. The last time we'd poked around in George Baker's business, it hadn't ended well. For anyone. "We should think rationally about this," I said. "Just because you hate him—"

Daphne held up a sheaf of papers. "Oh yeah? How about just because this is a big pile of research analyzing the value of the Haunted Village? You tell me, why would he need that unless he's helping someone buy up the land? *Again.*"

"There could be a lot of reasons," I said . . . though I couldn't exactly name one.

Daphne was searching methodically, drawer by drawer. I asked what she was looking for, but she said she'd know it when she saw it. And then she did: a small leather datebook.

"Who keeps a calendar on paper anymore?" I asked.

"Old people," Daphne said, flipping through. "Look—here's the date of the accident."

The entry read: Meet J and D at Lulu's Café.

"There are a lot of restaurants with that name," I said, my heart sinking.

"Yeah, including the restaurant on Main Street," Daphne said. She flipped more pages. "And look, he came back a month later, and a month after that. How come? Not because he was here with my mother to see me, I can tell you that much. So why? And why come in secret? Why's he here *now*?"

"He's here because your mother volunteered to stay with you while your dad's out of town," I reminded her.

"Yeah, so she *claims*. But doesn't this make more sense?"

"More sense than your mother wanting to take care of you?"

"Why would she start now?" Daphne said. Her face was ashen. I realized that for all her big talk, she hadn't wholly believed that her stepfather could be involved in this, that her mother could be married to a man like that—until now. "What if I'm right, V? What if it really is him?"

The night feels endless, as endless as the work. He is alone in his office, alone in the building, alone in the Haunted Village. Its fate rests on his shoulders, and he will carry the burden. He is the manager, and this title defines his entire being: He will *manage. As he always has.*

He is disliked. He knows that. He is harsh, but only because he has to be. Only because there are so many details, so many things to be done and so many things to go wrong, and only he knows them all. Only he can manage. His employees don't understand how much weight he carries. He is so tired.

So, so tired.

He rests his head on his desk for just a moment, and conjures a vision of the anniversary festival, perfect in every aspect. He will bring it to life. He will cross every item off his to-do list. He will ensure every employee perfectly performs. He will scare away any thoughts of actual haunting. He will let nothing interfere. He will—

He bolts upright, jolted from drowsiness by a flashing light. Something is out there in the dark, something that shouldn't be.

Something moaning, loud enough he can hear it from the safety of his office. The wind, he thinks.

But there is no wind tonight.

He does not want to go out there. He does not want to investigate, to ask a question and get an answer from the night.

But this is his job—this is his *place, and he will do his duty. He ventures outside.*

The sky is on fire.

He blinks. Rubs his eyes. Not possible. He is a rational man. A careful man. And yet—

Lights swirl, an aurora of reds and pinks and oranges, all of them streaming from the Vanishing Tree, and what looks like—

No. He backs away from the face emerging from the swirl of lights, backs straight into a brick wall, can back away no farther, is trapped by what cannot be but is: a spirit, lunging out of the night, reaching for him, mouth gaping open. When it speaks, he can feel the hot wind of it on his face.

YOU SHALL NOT BETRAY OUR MEMORY

YOU SHALL NOT DANCE ON OUR GRAVES

He squeezes his eyes shut, heart a drumbeat of terror, legs quivering, lungs too airless to scream.

YOU SHALL NOT

YOU SHALL NOT

YOU SHALL HEED OUR WARNING

OR FACE YOUR DOOOOOOOOOM

And then it is coming for him, it is reaching toward him, and he flings himself backward, cracks head into brick, gasps with the pain of it, as the bright lights blot out the world, and he orders himself to hang on, to defend this ground, to manage this situation, to manage, but he is so tired.

And it would be so easy, he thinks.

It would feel so good.

To let the darkness claim him.

To let go.

DAPHNE

I WAS DREAMING ABOUT an earthquake. When I woke up, the pillow was shaking. For a second, still half-asleep, I freaked out. Then I realized my phone was beneath my pillow, vibrating.

I groaned. Velma. Of course.

"You know it's the middle of the night, right?" I said, when I picked up.

"It's eight a.m.," she said.

"Exactly."

"There's been another ghost sighting, Daphne."

I bolted upright. "What?"

"Jerry got so spooked that he gave himself a concussion. They've closed the Haunted Village. And they're canceling the festival." Velma said she'd heard the whole story from her mom. There'd been some emergency meeting of the town council. According to the mayor, it was too dangerous to hold the anniversary festival until everything got sorted out. He didn't exactly say he *believed* that angry ghosts would bring doom raining down on us. But we both knew plenty of people did.

"This town is losing its mind," Velma said.

"What else is new? And more importantly, why am I losing sleep over it?"

"This is all connected. It has to be," Velma said, and explained that the town council was in wall-to-wall meetings about zoning restrictions. Dull-as-dirt details, but I got the point. Pretty soon, the Haunted Village would get sold off and turned into a condo complex, along with the rest of town. And I was willing to bet anything that my stepfather was drooling to do the deal.

I didn't care. Not about any of it, except for how it connected back to Marcy. And Velma was right, it had to. Somehow.

"We should talk to Dr. Hunter," Velma said.

"You're kidding."

"This is all connected to the town's history somehow. He might know something. And then we should go over to the Haunted Village, look for clues."

"We're not going to find any answers at the stupid library or the Haunted Village, Velma. This has my stepfather written all over it. We should follow him, catch him red-handed." And then I could grab him by the shoulders and shake him until a confession spilled out. Maybe then I could do the same to my mother, except in that case I'd be shaking sense into her, making her realize what kind of man she'd chosen over her family.

Was it worth it? I would ask. *Giving up your daughter for* that*?*

"We have our library shift today," Velma said, and I could tell there were plenty of things she was trying *not* to say. Her poker voice wasn't any better than her poker face. "Can we just talk to Dr. Hunter, go take a look at the Haunted Village for clues, and then I swear, we can start digging into your stepfather?"

I paused, thinking.

"I just want to make sure we cover all the bases," Velma said. "For Marcy's sake."

That's what mattered, I reminded myself. Not being right. Not making my mother see reality. Finding Marcy. Getting her back. Whatever it took.

"For Marcy's sake. Fine."

* * *

It was a struggle, pretending to be interested in anything Dr. Hunter had to say. But Velma had persuaded me to make the effort. He knew everything there was to know about the history of the town, she'd insisted. If anything like this—like, say, ghost sightings, poltergeists, people getting scared out of their minds at the thought that the original settlers were rising from their graves to visit doom on Crystal Cove—had happened before, Dr. Hunter would know.

And that would be useful to us, Velma kept saying, although I wasn't sure how—unless the ghost was an actual ghost, which it obviously was not. (I was almost definitely sure it was not.)

Any information is better than no information, Velma pointed out. She was, as usual, right. I'd forgotten how irritating that was. And how comforting.

I was taking my comfort wherever I could find it, especially as things started to feel more and more out of control. Marcy had been missing for weeks, and as far as I could tell, Velma and I were the only ones in town bothering to look for her. (Okay, Shaggy would have helped, if we'd let him, but as far as I was concerned, two people were a team, three were a crowd. Especially when the hypothetical third never left home without his dog and his appetite.)

On top of everything else, Dr. Hunter was late. When he finally showed up, it was just to grab his briefcase and leave again—"I can trust the two of you to hold down the fort in my absence, yes?" he said. "Something's come up at home."

"Can we just talk to you for a sec before you go?" Velma asked. "We have some questions about town history."

He looked like he wanted to blow her off, which blew my

mind. As far as I could tell, Dr. Hunter had never met a question he didn't want to answer with a hundred-hour-long, mind-numbingly boring lecture. "All right," he said, finally. "Just one sec, as you say."

"I wanted to ask you about the hauntings," Velma said.

He laughed. "Things are getting rather creepy, eh? Emma's threatening to move us out of town if this continues, and I suspect she's not the only one. This town prefers its frightening history to stay in the past."

"That's actually what I wanted to ask you about," Velma said. "Has something like this ever happened before?"

"Oh, mass hysteria is quite common in our nation's sordid history," Dr. Hunter said. "Just look at the Salem witch trials—" He launched into a lecture about the innocent women who'd been burned at the stake—leave it to Dr. Hunter to make even that sound boring—and I could tell that he would keep talking forever if we let him. Judging from the spellbound look on Velma's face, she'd be happy to listen.

I cleared my throat. "Uh, Dr. Hunter? We were actually more interested in *local* history."

He paused, then nodded. "Yes, there was an episode about a century ago—a con man came through town and faked a series of hauntings. Rather persuasively, according to the record."

"Why would he do that?" I asked.

"Because he was selling the frightened residents his services as an exorcist, and I gather he made a tidy bit of money—not to mention scared more than a few families into leaving town for good—before he got caught."

Velma snorted. "I can't believe people would give up their homes because they thought a *ghost* wanted them to."

"And why not?"

"Well, because . . . okay, it's one thing to believe that ghosts are maybe possible. But to be so absolutely sure that you'd ruin your life over it?"

"How can you be so certain they were ruining their lives?" he asked. "Perhaps their fear was simply giving them permission to do something they'd always wanted to do."

I'd never thought about it that way before. I guess Velma was right—even improbable things were still possible. Because who ever thought Dr. Hunter could manage to actually say something *interesting*?

"Maybe some of them," Velma said. "But I bet it's like you said, some of them were just scared. And I don't get how anyone could be that scared over *nothing*."

"Something you'll come to understand as you get older, Ms. Dinkley, is that people believe exactly what they want to believe—and they want most of all to believe in their own fears. If, for example, someone suspects the world is a dangerous place—and it would be foolish, these days, not to believe that—all it takes is a little push in the right direction to persuade them that they're right."

* * *

After Dr. Hunter left, we hung around and waited for a few minutes, just to be safe. Then we got to work. No, not the stupid photocopying he'd assigned us. I mean real work. The kind that actually mattered.

We moved some piles around so it looked like we'd accomplished something, so Dr. Hunter wouldn't know we'd skipped out on his precious filing. Next stop: the Haunted Village, which was officially shut down for the season. Not a problem for those of us with a key. Or at least, those of us with a partner with a key who was willing to use it.

We figured the place would be deserted, but as we approached the gate, we spotted a clump of girls using a tape measure to mark out a large patch of dirt. I recognized them from school—Thorn, Luna, and Dusk, wearing all black, with black lipstick and nail polish to match, as usual.

Those weren't their real names, of course. When we were all kids, they were just Sally, Kim, and Muffy. Then they formed their band: the Hex Girls.

Thorn, who was pretty quiet at school but a wild woman onstage, played the guitar and did most of the singing. She'd walked with a limp ever since we were kids, but no one knew why—no one I knew, at least.

Luna, on keyboards, was the most social one—she played soccer, she was president (and founder) of the high school's African American Student Association, and she was so cool, she even showed up at Fred's house after school sometimes.

Then there was Dusk, on the drums. Dusk had a temper, wore fake vampire fangs, and carried her drumsticks with her everywhere, just in case she needed to hit something. For a girl who always wore her hair in pigtails, she was more than a little terrifying.

The three of them had this whole witch/vampire/goth thing going, like it wasn't enough to love their music (which I kind of did), you also had to believe, or pretend you believed, they were creatures from the dark beyond (which I did not). I thought they were pretentious, to be honest. And I was pretty sure they thought I was drop-dead boring.

"What are you doing?" I asked when we got close enough.

All three of them ignored me. It's not that the Hex Girls were mean, exactly. They just didn't bother to be nice to anyone who didn't interest them. I kind of respected it. And I couldn't help noticing that Thorn seemed pretty interested in Velma. She was staring at her—and blushing.

"Hi," she said—to *Velma* only, it was pretty clear—and you could practically see her batting her eyelashes. "You coming to the midnight concert, Dink?"

"What concert?" I asked.

Again: totally ignored. I nudged Velma. *Dink.*

"Uh, what concert?" Velma echoed.

"We decided our ancestors deserve a celebration no matter what. So we're going to do a midnight concert on the anniversary—we can't get inside the gates, but we figure as long as we're in sight of the Vanishing Tree, it's all good." Thorn pointed up, where the tree's canopy was poking over the gates. "Just measuring out the space we need for a stage."

"You're not worried about the 'ghost'?" Velma asked.

"Music soothes the savage spirit, right?" Thorn said, winking. The other girls pretended not to be eavesdropping, but I could see they were lapping up every word. "Anyway, you should come, Dink. You can probably even score a backstage pass. I know a guy." She winked again.

Velma shrugged and said maybe—the kind of maybe that was pretty obviously an *over my dead body but thanks for asking*—and you could see Thorn's heart collapsing in on itself. At least, I could see it. Velma looked clueless.

"Okay, well, good luck!" she said, and started to walk away.

"Wait! Where are you going?"

"Uh . . ." Velma looked at me. The girl was a hopeless liar.

"We have to pick something up inside the park for Velma's mom. Official business," I said.

Now the Hex Girls were ready to acknowledge my existence. Their heads all swiveled toward me in sync.

"You can get in?" Thorn said.

"Yeah, totally." I could read her expression like a picture book—it was a combination of *I picked the wrong girl to flirt with* and *maybe it's not too late.* I grinned. Sometimes mean was fun. "*Velma and I* can get in. You can't. Sorry!"

I grabbed Velma's hand and pulled her away, fast, before they could bother trying to follow us inside the park.

The key got us through the gate, just as she'd promised. And just as she'd promised, there were no alarms or guard dogs or anything to stop us from going inside. "She's kind of cute, don't you think?" I said.

"Who?"

"Uh, Thorn? The girl who was practically begging you to make out with her back there?"

Velma blushed fiercely. "No way."

"Oh yes. All the way."

"Not exactly my type," Velma said, though I could tell she was flattered.

"What exactly is your type, anyway?" I asked, suddenly curious. I'd never really thought about it before.

"Well—guys."

"Care to be more specific?"

She shook her head. "No one around here, trust me."

"Okay, but let's say you were, like, trapped in Crystal Cove forever—"

Velma shuddered. "Don't even say those words."

"—who would you settle for? Who's the hottest—or the cutest—or, I don't know, the most sparkling personality, if that's your thing." I considered that. "Although come on, that's no one's thing."

"I don't know . . ."

"Mark? Howie? Marshall? Fred—"

My jaw dropped. At Fred's name, her face had turned tomato red.

"Fred?" I said, incredulous. "I never thought you'd be so conventional."

"Can we just go look for clues now?" Velma begged.

"We're just getting started!"

"Okay, so—who's *your* type?"

That's when the last face I expected—or wanted—to see popped unbidden into my head. I shook it away. Firmly. "No comment," I said. "Let's go find some clues."

* * *

We examined the managers' office, but there was nothing useful in there. So then we scanned the ground where Jerry had supposedly seen the ghost. We found . . . dirt.

"So you believe this guy, too? You think he saw . . . something?" I knew it wasn't a ghost, couldn't be a ghost. But the options for what it could have been seemed pretty sparse.

"I loathe Jerry," Velma admitted, "but if the Haunted Village goes down, his job goes with it. He'd have no incentive to make up a story like this, much less give himself a concussion."

"Okay, so, let's discuss: How do all these apparently sane people spontaneously start believing they saw a ghost? You think someone's wandering around in a white sheet shouting *Boo!*?"

"Not that, but . . . maybe, I don't know. Holograms? Lasers?" Velma was poking around in the roots of the Vanishing Tree, like she thought she'd find a microscopic holographic projector hidden in a squirrel's nest or something.

All I found were some crushed yellow flower petals, which was weird only because there were no yellow flowers anywhere in sight. I pointed them out to Velma. Her eyes widened. "Those are the same ones I found in Marcy's apartment," she said.

"Marcy never kept flowers in her apartment. She's got bad allergies."

Velma pulled out one of the plastic baggies she'd brought and scooped the petals into it. Our first official clue. Somehow it didn't give me very much hope.

"Can we stop wasting time and cut to the part where we follow my stepfather until we catch him in the act?" I said.

"We don't want to leap to the wrong conclusion, Daphne—all the evidence we have on him is circumstantial."

"Did you not hear Dr. Hunter? This is *just* like that con-man thing—scare people into selling off their property, collect the profits. Get out of town. A child could connect the dots."

"So how does Marcy fit in?" Velma pressed.

"That's my point. That's what we have to find out!"

"Daphne, has it occurred to you that . . ." She pressed her lips together, like she was trying to hold something in.

"What?"

She shook her head.

"*What.* Just say it."

She caved. "Okay, I'm just thinking—if Marcy was working for this mystery guy, whether or not it was your stepfather, have you thought about the possibility that she was doing it voluntarily? That maybe whatever's going on here, Marcy's in on it? Maybe she did run away, but because she was worried about getting caught? This whole thing—the 'fake' runaway note, Marcy getting so publicly upset, swearing she was going to confess, all of it—what if it was just an act?"

No. I would not even consider this. And I certainly wouldn't allow Velma, who barely knew Marcy, who didn't even *like* Marcy, to consider it. "That's not possible."

"Sherlock Holmes said that once you eliminate the impossible—"

"I don't care who said what. Marcy *wouldn't.* I thought you were on my side here," I said. "I thought you cared about finding her!"

"I care about finding the truth," Velma said. "Marcy's a part of that, yes. But this is bigger than just her. This is about the Haunted Village, the town, the people who live here—and I'm just saying we have to consider all the options."

"*I* don't have to consider anything."

"Well, maybe that's a sign your judgment is clouded," she said.

That turned my anger up to a boil. How dare she. How dare Velma, of all people, suggest that I didn't know my best friend well enough to know what she was capable of. How dare Velma pretend we were a team when all this time, she only cared about stupid real estate and her precious Haunted Village. "Maybe *your* judgment is clouded," I said.

"What's that supposed to mean? Excuse me if I care about my mother's job and the fate of this town and—"

"You can pretend that's what it's about, but we both know you hate Marcy," I said. "You're probably wishing she'd stay gone forever, because that's the only way for you to finally get a friend. Pathetic."

She flinched. Good.

"I knew it," she said, and I could tell she was trying not to cry.

Even better.

I was being a monster, I knew that. And because of it, for the first time since Marcy disappeared, I could stop feeling sad and scared and alone—I felt nothing but anger. It was a huge relief.

"You knew what?" I snarled.

"I knew this was the real you. Ugly and mean. People think you're so nice, but they don't know you like I do. I stupidly let myself believe you'd changed—or that I was wrong about you. I stupidly let myself forgive you, even though you never said you're sorry."

I forced myself to laugh. "Like you're even capable of forgiveness. Look at you, holding a grudge for something that happened when we were ten years old. You tell yourself this story of how you're all alone in the world because your best friend dumped you? We were *ten*! Does it seem normal to you, letting that be the reason for the rest of your life? You just want someone to blame for being all alone. But it's your fault you're alone, Velma. It's your choice. You're alone because you're too scared to be anything else."

"You're not even capable of being sorry, are you." Velma's voice was colder than I'd ever heard it. Flat. Dead.

I'd done that to her.

I tried not to let myself feel guilty. I was so tired of feeling.

"You claim Marcy's your best friend?" Velma said. "I don't think you even know what that means." She walked off and left me there, alone, just like everyone always did, eventually.

I hated her. That's what I told myself.

Tried to tell myself.

She was wrong. She was so far off base about everything that she wasn't even on the field. She was wrong about Marcy, and she was wrong about me. Every word out of her mouth, wrong.

Except for one thing.

It was true: I'd never told her I was sorry. I'd never found the nerve.

VELMA

I LOCKED THE GATES. I walked home. I commanded myself, with each trudging step: *Don't cry. Don't cry.* I had sworn I would never again cry over Daphne Blake. Like I'd sworn I would never let myself believe in anyone again like I'd once believed in Daphne. Except here I was again, a total idiot, paying the price for believing in someone—and not just someone like Daphne, but Daphne herself. Fool me once, shame on you. Fool me twice, I figured I must have been the biggest idiot on the planet.

I'd let myself go soft.

I'd let myself—and I could admit it now that it was over—imagine some fairy-tale future where the two of us were friends again, for real. Like that would ever have worked. Especially once Marcy came back.

At that thought, I stopped cold. Because that was another thing I could only admit now, and only on a deserted street, all alone with no one to peer inside my head and guess at the ugly secrets inside: It was possible that Daphne was just a little bit right. Marcy's disappearance had made my life better. It had brought Daphne back to me . . . and I'd enjoyed it. I liked teaming up with her, I liked trying to solve a mystery again . . . did that mean I liked Marcy being gone? And that I wanted her to stay that way? Could I really be that terrible a person?

I didn't think so, or at least, I didn't want to think so. Just like I didn't want to think Daphne could be right about any of the other horrible things she'd said. Like how I was desperate to blame someone for my life when the only person to blame was myself. Like how I was scared of having friends, because caring about someone included the risk of losing them, and I was scared to get hurt again. Because deep down, I knew it was easier to be alone.

And it was certainly easier than this. This hurt.

I took out my phone, opened the messaging app, and let my finger hover over Daphne's name. I could text her and . . . what? Not apologize, certainly, because I hadn't done anything wrong. I was mostly sure of that.

As I was wondering what that left to say, and why I felt so driven to say it, the phone buzzed in my hand. In my surprise, I almost dropped it, but managed to answer before it went to voice mail. Unknown number.

"Hello?"

At the sound of a man's voice, my heart dropped, and I realized I'd been hoping it was somehow Daphne.

"Milford Jones here, with some information you're going to want. I did some digging into your supposed grand theft auto, and couldn't find any record of it anywhere, which—"

"My source is trustworthy, Mr. Jones. It happened."

"Hold your horses, young lady."

I hated the patronizing way he talked to me as much as I hated everything else about this guy, but I held them.

"I was going to say, which seemed *suspicious* to me, because I often find that a good story is usually a true story."

I bet you do, I thought. I was still half-convinced this guy was our best suspect, but if he had information that could be useful, I wanted to hear it.

"You were right about the police report," he continued. "Wiped clean. But her name's still in the system—harder to wipe the record of a file than it is to wipe its contents. So I was able to deduce some of the other variables, timing, personnel, and I'm not going to reveal too much about how the sausage is made, but if I do say so myself—"

"Do you have a name for me, Mr. Jones?"

There was a long, disappointing pause.

"Well, now you've spoiled the fun," he said. "No, I couldn't get a name."

I deflated. When would I learn my lesson about hoping?

"I do hate to disappoint a lady, though—so what I have for you is the year and make of the car."

It was something, at least. I scrambled for a pen and my notebook to write down the details: cherry-red 1973 Ford Mustang. "It's better than nothing," I told him, and tried to keep the giddiness out of my voice. It was substantially better than nothing, but I suspected he'd be more useful if he thought he needed to impress me.

"Better than nothing, she says? When I produce not just a rabbit out of a hat, but a rabbit out of midair? No hat!" He sighed dramatically. "You think I'm done? Milford Jones is never done until he gets his scoop. More soon, little lady, and then I look forward to getting the scoop from you and your partner."

The phone went dead. I was about to text my partner to tell her we'd finally gotten a break in the case—when I remembered. We weren't partners anymore. Daphne didn't want my help.

It didn't mean I needed to stop investigating—it just meant I didn't need her help anymore. This was the proof. It would also be proof that Daphne was wrong; I *did* care about finding Marcy. Just like I cared about my mother's job, and the Haunted Village, and the people of

Crystal Cove who were getting duped into terror.

The only thing I absolutely refused to care about, ever again, was Daphne Blake.

* * *

I couldn't fall asleep that night, and after a few fruitless hours of tossing, turning, and brooding, I gave up.

Instead, I got to work: First I tried to figure out how to search car ownership data online, but I couldn't find anything accessible to the public. Then I tried scanning Google Maps street shots of Crystal Cove, to see if I could spot the red Mustang parked in front of someone's house. This was also a huge waste of time.

Finally, I skimmed through database after database of flower species, trying to identify the yellow petals that kept turning up, but that was a dead end, too. There was no way to match crushed pieces of blossom to the photos of whole, intact flowers.

Everything felt like a waste of time. I gave up on the case, for the moment, and gave in to temptation. Under my bed was a shoebox full of photos I never let myself look at, a record of my old friendship with Daphne. I sorted through the box slowly—not just photos, but also movie tickets, even some candy wrappers, a reminder of some inside joke I'd long since forgotten. There was an official disciplinary slip from the elementary school principal, and that one I did remember—a boy in art class called me ugly, and Daphne reciprocated by dumping a bucket of paint in his lap. Which was when he called her stupid, and I dumped a second bucket of paint on him, staining his hair perma-pink. He came to school the next day with a shaved head. Daphne and I spent every afternoon that week in the principal's office, getting lectures on how two wrongs didn't make a right.

It was the first time I'd ever gotten in trouble, but I didn't care. I just felt guilty that Daphne had to suffer along with me—I told her she shouldn't have bothered to get involved; it's not like the boy had said anything untrue.

"I know I'm not pretty," I told Daphne.

"You're an idiot," she said. Then she said that I was the one who should have just let it go after he called her stupid, because maybe it was true.

"You're *not* an idiot. You're the smartest person I know, other than me," I told her. "Why else would you be my best friend?"

We agreed: Anyone who wanted to insult one of us better watch out for the other one (and any nearby buckets of paint). Best friends forever, we swore, and it was the kind of thing you said when you were a kid—but I'd believed it.

But forever had lasted about three more months, and I stopped believing in much of anything then.

Jinkies crawled into my lap, like she knew I needed something to hold on to. I held tight. Rubbed my cheek against her fur. Felt just a little bit less alone. I yawned, wondering why I was torturing myself with any of this. "What do you think, Jinkies?" I asked. "Should I just give up?"

"I'm thinking no." My mother poked her head into the room. "Giving up doesn't sound much like your style." Jinkies meowed, as if to say she agreed. "Shouldn't you have been asleep about four hours ago?"

"Shouldn't you?" I countered.

She came into the room, two mugs of hot chocolate in her hands—she gave one to me. I cupped it gratefully, warmth seeping into my whole body. "I can't sleep when I know something's wrong with my favorite daughter."

"Your only daughter."

"¿Y? Does that matter?" She sat down on the bed beside me. "You want to talk about it?"

I sipped the hot chocolate. She'd added cinnamon, just the way I liked it. I didn't want to worry her. But I also didn't want to drown. "I just . . . I feel like everything's going wrong," I admitted. "You're about to lose your job, the Village is going to close, the town will lose everything—"

"Whoa! Where's all this coming from?"

"Uh, you?" I wondered if she thought I'd been tuning her out all this time, if her doom and gloom ranting about Crystal Cove's future had bounced off me without making a dent.

"Mi amor." She put an arm around me, and I relaxed into her. "That's my fight, not yours. I know I can sound a little alarmist—"

"A *little*?"

"That's only because I'm trying to wake people up, to make them understand what the worst-case scenario looks like, so we can avoid it. But that's not what I want for you, thinking that the worst is always just around the corner. Things are going to be okay, Velma, te lo prometo."

"Dad?" I said, before I could think better of it. "Will Dad be okay?"

My mother's arm stiffened around me for a moment, then tugged me in tighter. "He's working on it, hon. That's all we can ask."

"Sometimes I think, if we hadn't lost the museum, the house, if things had just stayed the way they were, he wouldn't have . . ."

"That was all so long ago, Velma—is that really what has you up all night? Looking like you lost your best friend?"

I choked back a sob. I refused to start crying, especially now. It was selfish, asking my mother to comfort me when she was dealing with so much more. "Just tell me, what will happen to us, worst-case scenario. If you lose your job, if the town starts selling off all its land . . . will we have to move?"

"Crystal Cove is our home," my mother said. "We're not going anywhere."

"Do you ever think . . . maybe it would be better to leave? Make a fresh start somewhere else?"

My mother faced me with a fierce look. "This is my

home, Velma. Someday, you'll grow up and go somewhere far away—" She must have been able to tell I was about to interrupt, to deny it, because she pressed a soft finger to my lips. "I know you. And I know your heart's dreaming bigger dreams than Crystal Cove. That's good! That's how I raised you, to dream big. But that's what Crystal Cove is for me—my dream. I'm not abandoning it, now or ever."

It was something I had never understood. She'd given so much to this place, year after year. "Why? How can you love something when it pretty clearly doesn't love you back?"

"Mira, have I ever told you that when your father and I got married, we almost settled in Los Angeles instead of here in Crystal Cove?"

"No! Really?"

She nodded. "That was the original plan—LA was the only home I'd ever known. I grew up with my parents telling me every day how lucky I was to live there. How they'd emigrated from Mexico months before I was born and built this wonderful life for themselves in the greatest city on earth. Your father was willing to move there, for me.

"Then I went with him to visit his hometown, and I fell in love with it, just the way I'd fallen in love with him. Crystal Cove felt like home to me in a way LA never had. You know how you feel, wanting something bigger? Maybe I wanted something smaller, something built on a human scale. So I adopted it as my home, and I've fought for it ever since.

"You know what someone told me, at the first protest I went to here? 'What do you care, this town doesn't belong to you!' They didn't care that I thought it was my home. They just cared that I was an outsider. And I've been fighting that, too, ever since."

"I don't get it, then. Why would you fight for a place that keeps making you feel like you don't belong?"

"Velma, people have been trying to make me feel like that for my entire life. But they're only going to succeed if I let them. No one but me gets to decide where I belong—and I belong here. I love the desert, I love the sea, I love the history, and I love the people—not all of them, but enough of them. That's why your father's so obsessed with that mythical land deed—it's not for him; it's for me. He wants me to feel entitled to be here. He's never fully understood: I don't need a piece of paper giving me permission to belong here. This is a town built by immigrants, built by people looking for a place to call home—people who didn't have any more or less right to be here than I do. Some people would rather forget that history, and that's another reason I fight. I want Crystal Cove to stay in the hands of the people who remember. I'm fighting for what I love. Just like you, Velma."

"I don't think I'd be tough enough for a fight like that," I said.

"¿Tú?" The most stubborn girl I know?" She stood up and

gave me a soft kiss on the forehead. "You don't give up on a fight, Velma. You don't give up on anything."

She turned the lights off on her way out, and I got the message—I lay down in bed, tried, once again, to sleep.

I couldn't stop thinking about it, though. The idea that I was some kind of stubborn fighter who didn't give up. That's who I wanted to be.

But what if Daphne was right? What if all those years ago, I didn't just give up on her—I gave up on myself?

DAPHNE

AFTER THE FIGHT, I drove. I drove in circles for hours, trying not to think about the fight.

Thinking about the fight.

When I finally made it home, still fuming, I was an hour later than I was supposed to be. Which my mother pointed out the moment I walked through the door. She and my stepfather were sitting on the couch reading, while the girls sat at their feet, playing with a puzzle. It was a disgustingly cozy image of a perfect family . . . that I wasn't a part of.

"Fine, send me to my room. But you're about six years later than *you're* supposed to be," I snapped back. "So where are you sending yourself?"

"Do we have to leave?" one of the twins yelped, looking at our mother in panic.

"We like it here!" the other said, and you could tell from the wobble in her voice that the waterworks were coming soon. Great.

"Of course you don't have to leave," George told them. "Your sister's just throwing a bit of a tantrum."

It was bad enough that Velma had made me feel like I was ten years old again. That after all this time, everything had come full circle, that I was still the person who would vomit all that ugliness onto someone I cared about, that I'd learned nothing, fixed nothing, that I was a person destined to screw up every friendship I ever had—bad enough, but I could handle it, all of it.

What I could not handle was George, the person responsible for ruining my life the first time around, the person I was pretty sure was responsible yet again, sitting in *my* house, with the family that should have been *mine*, and telling me I was acting like a child.

"Don't you dare talk about me like I'm not here," I said to him, ice-cold. "And don't you dare act like you know anything about me or why I might be angry. Did it occur to you I'm angry because destroying my life once wasn't enough for you? Destroying my father's life wasn't enough for you? You have to come back here and try to destroy the whole town? Not to mention my best friend?"

"Girls, go upstairs," he said, and the girls made a run for it.

"What's she talking about?" my mother asked. "What do you have to do with her friend?" Now she was talking about me in the third person, too. When had I turned invisible? How loud and how angrily did I have to shout before she remembered that I existed—that I was right here in front of her?

"Yeah, George, what do you have to do with Marcy? You want to tell your wife how you've been sneaking into town all these months? Having secret meetings? Putting together some kind of super sketchy con, so you can spook people into doing what you want?"

"Daphne, you don't know what you're talking about," my stepfather said, and he didn't sound defensive, he just sounded tired. Like I was exhausting him. I wouldn't have thought it was possible to get any angrier, but here I was.

Angrier.

"It's not a secret that your stepfather's recently been in town on some business," my mother said. Of course she would defend him. Of course she would pick him over me.

"Oh yeah? What business?" I said. "Who are your clients?"

"You know I can't tell you that," he said.

"Attorney-client privilege," my mother added.

"How convenient." I hated him. In that moment, I hated him more than I'd ever hated anyone—except for her. And it suddenly occurred to me that she was probably in on it, too. "Dad may be naive enough to think you're a good person—but I should have known better. There's no way you would come here just for me."

"Daphne, you don't mean that," she said.

"You don't know me well enough to know what I mean," I said. It was all coming out, finally, all the terrible things I'd been trying so long not to say. "And that's because you picked him over me. You met him while he was trying to ruin someone's life, and somehow, you fell in love with that—so excuse me for thinking you might be just as terrible as he is. You'd have to be, to do what you did. To leave."

She went pale. Opened her mouth, but nothing came out. Her husband spoke for her. "Daphne, you have no idea what you're—"

But she stopped him. "George, give us some time alone, please."

"I don't want time alone," I said, but of course, he listened to her, not to me. And then there were two.

"So what do you want?" she asked me, once it was just us.

"From you?" I wanted the last six years back. I wanted our family back. I wanted her to go back in time and make a different choice. I wanted her to stay. "I want *nothing*." But it didn't come out the way I'd intended it to come out, like a knife stabbing through her heart. It came out like a sob, and then, before I could stop it, there was a flood of tears.

I did not want to cry, and I definitely did not want my mother to put her arms around me, to wrap me in a bear hug, squeeze tight, promise me that I was loved, that I was cared for, that I would be okay; I did not want that to feel good, to feel like the one thing I'd been longing for all these years. I did not want it to feel like coming home.

"I love you, Daphne," she whispered, over and over again.

I always thought the part of myself that missed my mother was weak—but maybe it wasn't so weak after all, because it won out.

"I love you, too."

* * *

I don't know why it's always easier to talk in the dark, but it's a fundamental fact of reality. And my mother and I were both realists. So we sat at the kitchen table, lights off, a lavender-scented candle flickering between us, and we talked. We talked for real, for the first time I could remember. Maybe the first time ever.

"You were too young then to really explain things to," my mother said quietly. She kneaded her fingers together, nervously. "Or we thought you were. Maybe that was our mistake. One of them. I made a lot of them, back then."

"Like cheating on Dad." I didn't say it to be mean. I just said it because it seemed like another fact of reality. And maybe because I wanted to know what she would say—whether she thought it was a mistake.

She looked down at her fingers, untangled them. "I'm not proud of that. But you should know, Daphne, George isn't the reason our marriage ended. Things were over before I met him—your father and I had already decided to separate. We were just working out the details of custody, housing . . . when you've been together for that long, when you planned to stay together forever, it's complicated. Disentangling. The funny thing is, it was the first thing in a long time we'd done together. We were actually getting along."

I remembered that—for a year or two, it seemed like my parents were constantly fighting. Then that summer, the fighting had finally ended. I assumed it meant they were happy again, and would have been happy for good, had George Baker not screwed everything up.

"It helped that we were both in agreement," she continued. "We didn't want you growing up like that, in a house filled with anger. We wanted to end things before we lost any shred of caring about each other. The thing with George, it was just supposed to be a distraction, and your father knew about it—"

"Wait." My mind basically exploded. "What?"

"He knew," she repeated. "I told him, and he understood. It was a hard time, for both of us, and . . . he understood."

All this time, I'd thought my mother was the villain, my father the innocent victim. And I'd also thought that just maybe, if Velma had never caught my mother with another man, or never told me about it, or if I'd never confronted my mother about it, then maybe my parents would have just stayed together.

I'd thought it was my fault.

"I loved your father," she said. "Marrying him wasn't a mistake—but splitting up wasn't a mistake, either. And I think he'd tell you the same thing. I never expected George to turn into anything real, but when he did . . . you know, your father called me, the day before the wedding? He told me he was happy for me, that he hoped I'd be happy with George. Not that I needed his permission to be happy, but I was glad I had it."

I didn't know what to say.

"My mistake was letting you imagine what happened instead of just telling you," she said. "And my biggest mistake of all was letting you push me away."

When they split up, my parents agreed on joint custody. I was the one who'd disagreed. Every time I had to leave for my mother's house, I threw a fit. Until finally, they both stopped making me go. I got exactly what I'd asked for. So I told myself it was what I'd wanted.

"I didn't want to see the look on your face," she said. "The one that said you hated me. It seemed easier to let you hate me from afar. And that's something I'll never forgive myself for."

"I never hated you," I admitted. "I just . . . I thought you didn't want me anymore. That you had your perfect family, and I was just, I don't know. A leftover."

"Oh, Daphne. You're no such thing." She grabbed my

hand, squeezed tight, and I let her. "You have no idea how important you are to me."

"So if you don't regret marrying Dad, and if I'm so important to you, and if you didn't leave because of George, then . . . why? Why did you leave him?"

"I loved your father, Daphne, I did. But we were so young when we met—I was here on summer vacation from college, with your aunt Emma. It was before I'd started the business, before I even knew who I was, really. We fell head over heels for each other. It was a summer fling—we never thought it would last."

"Maybe it shouldn't have."

"I'm glad it did," she said. "Because I have you. And I am so proud of who you've become."

"Shallow and mean?"

"Confident and outspoken and fiercely loyal," she countered. "And, I recognize this is going to sound a little like I'm giving myself a compliment, but—you remind me a lot of myself when I was your age."

"No way."

She got up and opened a kitchen drawer, the one where we'd once kept all our takeout menus. Last I checked, it was empty. "I want to show you something," she said. "I brought this from San Francisco, but I wasn't sure you'd want it."

She set a small, faded photo album in front of me. It was a dusty pink, its pages yellowing. I opened the front cover, and the first page was filled with photos of my mom, looking younger than I'd ever seen her before—maybe around my age, i.e., younger than I'd imagined it was possible for her to be.

"These are photos from that summer, when I came here and met your dad. I thought you might want to see who we were back then. Who I was. Maybe if you knew me a little better as a person, not just your mom, it might help you understand why I made some of the choices I did. I'm not perfect, Daphne." She ran her hands through her hair, just like I always did when I was trying to figure out exactly the right words to say. "I'm nowhere near perfect. But I want you to know those parts of me, too. The flaws. The mistakes. The whole picture. Only if you want to, of course."

I took the album. "I do."

She looked pointedly toward the stairs, up which my stepfather and half sisters had disappeared. "I'm not telling you what you should feel about George, or about your sisters—"

"They're not—"

"You're their big sister, like it or not. And, for the record," she said, "they worship you. So could you please just be a little kinder to them?"

I couldn't fathom the idea of them worshipping me, or even liking me that much. They were so perfect, so well behaved, such disgustingly sharp little geniuses—what would they possibly want with a big sister like me?

I liked the sound of it, though: *big sister.* I'd never really thought of myself as one of those before.

"George, on the other hand, is a grown man, who doesn't need me interfering on his behalf—so I'm going to trust that the two of you can work things out in your own time. But I want you to know, Daphne, he's a good man. Whatever it is you think he's up to, he's not. I wouldn't love him the way I do if he weren't a good man."

"What if you're wrong?" I asked her.

"What if you are?"

* * *

I apologized to the step-brats and promised them that no one was kicking them out of the house, especially me. I had to admit, they looked kind of cute, curled up together on the king-sized mattress in the guest room. Daisy asked if I would teach her how to braid her hair, and when I told her I would, Dawn asked if I could help her with her science project. I couldn't imagine why anyone, even a five-year-old, would want my help on a science project, but when I said yes, her whole face lit up.

Big sister: Maybe I could get used to that.

Apologizing to my stepfather was a slightly less adorable—and less appealing—proposition. I wasn't even sure I *wanted* to apologize—Velma, I had to admit, was right. All our evidence on him was circumstantial. But was I just supposed to take my mother's word for it that he was a good person? I'd spent half my life hating him. It was going to take more than one night to make an emotional U-turn.

Still. I found him in my father's office. I entered without knocking—it was, after all, still *my* father's office. But I didn't go any farther than the doorway. "I wanted to say I'm sorry, for the way I talked to you before," I said. It was excruciating. But it also felt like setting down something very heavy that I'd been carrying for a long time. "Actually, for the way I always talk to you."

"You want to say sorry?" he said, wryly. "Or your mother is making you say it?"

"I know you don't know me that well, but does it seem like I let people make me say things I don't mean?"

He laughed, and for a second it felt almost like there was something between us besides hostility. Almost as if he liked me, which didn't seem remotely possible. It had never occurred to me that *like* was a verb either of us would ever use with respect to the other.

George invited me to sit. "While you were downstairs, I spoke with my client to see whether they'd mind me sharing some of the details of the case with you, so I could explain why I've been coming to Crystal Cove so often recently."

That was unexpected. "Why would you do that?"

"For starters, because you accused me of trying to destroy the town and—if I'm reading between the lines correctly—kidnapping your best friend?"

Okay, so he was charming. I reminded myself to show no weakness. Be objective, gather evidence, that was my only job. "So what's the story?"

"You're right that there are some shadow investors looking to buy up land in Crystal Cove and doing their best to circumvent the zoning policies so they can do as they'd like with it. But I'm not working for them."

"Then who?"

"You're familiar with Citizens for Crystal Cove?"

My eyebrows nearly flew off my face. That was Velma's mother's group, the ones always staging protests at the mayor's office. "*That's* your client?"

"They hired me to do some digging, make sure nothing illegal's going on, and if it is, make sure we're positioned to get an injunction before any property changes hands. I know you blame me for . . . well, for a lot, Daphne. But this time, I'm fighting for the good guys. Get to know me a little—you might even decide I'm one of them."

"I guess anything's possible," I said, and couldn't suppress a smile.

The moment I got out of there, I whipped out my phone to call Velma and tell her that, even if I'd gotten things wrong about my stepfather, we were definitely right that some kind of shady real estate deal was behind all the fake hauntings. It's possible I wanted to tell her a lot more than that, because in a way, she was the only person who could understand what had just happened and how my entire picture of my family and my life story had just been turned inside out.

But then, phone in hand, I remembered. The things I'd said to her. The things she'd said to me. The distance between us, exploding into an impassable chasm just when it seemed like we might finally close it. I could suck it up and apologize, of course. I could even finally find the nerve to apologize for the way I'd treated her when we were kids, the way I'd treated her ever since. I wanted to. I'd wanted to for years.

But I didn't.

The moonglow showers her in silver light. She waits, heart thumping, tension building, the crowd a silent hush of shadowed faces, all of them tipped toward her. They are eager, they are impatient, they are in her thrall.

This is her favorite moment, the before. This is when she feels her witchiest, when she feels the power building, thrumming inside her, begging for release. Tonight, of all nights, she will play conduit to that power, unleash it to the heavens.

Silence, as the second hand ticks toward midnight.

Silence, as the anniversary nears. And then—

A wild howl breaks the stillness. She throws her head back, the howl surging through her, the microphone blasting it at the crowd. Then she signals her girls, and the music kicks in. It is time to rock the night.

They blast their music loud enough to wake the spirits, and their music is a song she wrote herself, a song for the vanished girls, the ones who came to a new land, built a life for themselves, raised children, buried husbands, lived and loved and dreamed and disappeared. There is an electric buzz on the breeze, and she can feel them, the spirits of all those girls, surrounding the crowd, cheering on the secret concert, and a part of her truly believes they're here, her ancestors, watching her.

The power of the stage gives her this power, too, the power to love being watched. At school she longs to be invisible, but here, she wants their eyes on her, past and present—she wants everyone to see her. Here she is magnetic, drawing their gazes, sucking their energy from them, firing it back, sparks from her fingers, from her heart, from her voice, she can almost see them, colors arcing across the sky, and . . .

She does *see them, a rainbow blaze of lights, swirling lights swooping at the crowd, and the music is drowned out by screams.*

A voice, and it is not her voice. It overwhelms her voice. It says YOU WERE WARNED . . . it says NOW YOU SHALL PAY and then there's a crack of blinding light, and her mouth is open, and she tries to scream.

But there is only silence.

VELMA

WHEN I CAME DOWN to breakfast, my parents were both already in the kitchen, which was weird, and they were both staring at the TV, which was weirder. My mom didn't believe in watching TV during meals. Or ever, basically.

"How could they just disappear?" my father was saying as I came in.

"What's going on?" I asked.

My mother was furiously dialing her phone. My father pointed limply at the screen. There was a reporter standing outside the Haunted Village, where I knew the Hex Girls had been planning to throw their anniversary concert the night before.

"They're gone," my father said quietly. "The band."

"The Hex Girls? What do you mean, 'gone'?"

“Witnesses say the concert was interrupted by a strange phenomenon of lights and voices in the sky, and in the midst of the chaos, all three members of the Hex Girls vanished,” the reporter on-screen said, sounding skeptical. “Many in the crowd, all of them local teens, claim to have seen a ghost.”

“It’s horrible, I know,” I heard my mother saying into the phone. “But it’s not just the girls—this will be the last straw for the town council, and the zoning vote is tomorrow; we’ve got to get on this.”

“I . . . uh . . . I have to go,” I said.

Nobody noticed. My father was mesmerized by the news report. My mother was wheeling and dealing on the protest circuit. There was no one to notice me slipping out the door, no one to say, *No, Velma, don’t, it’s not safe for girls out there anymore.*

It was useful, maybe, to be a ghost. That’s what I told myself. This was freedom. I had places to be, and it was a good thing no one wanted to stop me from being there, that no one was worried enough to care—or maybe, a little voice suggested, no one cared enough to worry.

It was a good thing.

* * *

All week I’d been thinking of the Haunted Village as *the scene of the crime*, but it was weird to see it as an actual crime scene, complete with flashing lights, yellow police tape, cops, reporters, and shell-shocked witnesses, all of them kids I recognized from school.

It was one thing to see a news story on TV. It was another to live inside it, come face-to-face with the fact that this was real. Thorn, Luna, and Dusk were gone. Who was I to think I could somehow bring them back, all on my own? It seemed ridiculous, and I could almost hear the third-grade jeers—Detective Dinkley saves the day—but I tried to ignore the echo. I was Detective Dinkley. I could save the day.

I couldn't get too close to the makeshift stage, and most of the witnesses were corralled with cops or reporters, but I found Haley Moriguchi kneeling by the edge of the front gate, tear-streaked and hyperventilating. I sat down beside her and, before I had time to think better of it, squeezed her hand.

"You doing okay, Haley?"

She turned to me, eyes wide, and I was assuming she'd demand to know what made me dare to imagine she'd want to talk to me, but instead, she hugged me. I let her.

"Velma, oh my god, it was awful," she said. "I wasn't even supposed to go to this stupid concert. My parents were afraid something would happen, but it's like, who believes in *ghosts*, right? Except now I do, I guess." She hiccuped.

"What exactly happened?" I asked gently.

"The sky turned all these colors, and this, like, spirit voice spoke to us and told us we were all going to be punished, and then they were just . . . *gone.* What if they never come back, Velma? What if this is how it happened the last time?"

"What?"

"The *Vanishing,*" she said, a little trace of her usual *you're an idiot* tone seeping in. That seemed like a good sign. "What if this is how it happened the last time, people just disappearing? What if we're next?"

"That can't be what's happening," I said. "I promise. We're going to figure this out."

I just wasn't sure how. Of course it wasn't a ghost, couldn't have been a ghost—and it certainly wouldn't have been that hard for a living, breathing human being to rig a trapdoor in a makeshift stage. Especially one like this, that even from here I could see had a hollow underneath. You could aim colored spotlights at the sky, you could even broadcast a ghostly voice, but how did you get a whole crowd of cynical teenagers to truly believe in a *ghost*?

I started poking around the fringes of the crime scene, staying away from the crowds and the panic, not even sure what I was looking for until I spotted it—crushed yellow flower petals. And this time, an actual intact flower! I snapped a picture with my phone and did an image search. It was a start, and maybe if I could figure out what was so special about this flower—

"Guess I should have known you'd be here, too."

I looked up in surprise. Daphne looked just as surprised

to see me. Not angry, at least—but not too pleased, either.

"I came as soon as I heard," I said. "I had to get a look."

"Me too," she admitted. "I can't believe they're gone."

"Just like Marcy," I said. And then, all in a rush, because doing things before I could think better of them seemed to be working for me: "You were right, Daphne. This is more important than real estate. This is about girls in trouble. Not just the Hex Girls. Marcy. That's what matters, finding them. I got carried away by the mystery of it, by the idea of cracking the case—"

"No," she said firmly. "You were right, trying to be objective. I'm the one who got carried away. I was so determined to see what I wanted to see, I was ready to ignore any evidence I didn't like. That doesn't help Marcy. It doesn't help anyone."

"I must be hearing things, because that almost sounded like an apology."

"It wasn't." She gave me a fierce glare—then it melted away into something much softer. "But this is: I'm sorry, V. I should never have accused you of not caring. Or any of those other things, about making yourself miserable, or whatever. That's none of my business."

"It's possible you were right," I admitted. As long as we were admitting things, it seemed like we might as well go all the way. "I had good reasons not to want any more friends . . . or at least, I thought they were good reasons. Now? I don't know. I feel like I don't know anything anymore."

"I'm so sorry, V. I should have said so before."

"Uh, you did say so before—like thirty seconds ago."

"No. Not about this." She had a very un-Daphne-like look on her face. Almost like she was nervous. "I mean, also about this. But I meant, I'm sorry for what happened when we were kids."

I couldn't believe it. I'd been waiting years for her to say that. And for most of those years, I'd imagined the way I would react, the way I would laugh in her face, tell her too little, too late, or maybe tell her I didn't even know what she was talking about, make her believe she was just as inconsequential to me as I was to her. But now that the moment was here, I didn't want to do any of it. I just wanted to listen.

"That's a cowardly way to put it," she continued. "Passive voice. 'What happened.' I'm sorry for what I *made* happen. For ditching you, for the things I said about you. I was just so angry about my mom—"

"I know."

"But I shouldn't have taken it out on you."

"Trust me, I know that, too."

"I wanted to apologize back then," Daphne said, and like I said, I don't know everything, because I never had a clue about that. "I couldn't figure out how to do it. Or maybe I was just scared. But I missed you so much. All this time."

"Why didn't you ever . . . ?"

"I figured you hated me," she said.

"I sort of did. But I guess . . ." If she could rip herself open and show me the secret inside, then maybe I owed it to her—or at least to myself—to do the same. "I missed you, too."

One of the police cars turned its siren on as it pulled out, and I suddenly remembered where we were, and why. It felt wrong, being this happy in the midst of all this panic and fear. But you can't help how you feel. We stared at each other, awkward now that the truth was out.

"I feel like we're probably supposed to hug now," she said, "but I know you hate that, so—"

I threw my arms around her, and for a few endless seconds we hung on like we were stranded in the middle of the ocean and it was the only way to stay afloat.

"So, partners again?" she asked when we finally let go.

"Partners," I said eagerly. "And look what I found!" I showed her the site I'd clicked on just as she showed up. It turned out the flower was a rare species of brugmansia, the same flower as in Aunt Emma's centerpiece. It was a variation known to cause hallucinations and a state of extreme suggestibility when ingested. It was especially potent when fresh blossoms were crushed and mixed with water, and then inhaled as a mist. "It sounds like if you got someone to breathe that in, all you'd have to do is *suggest* the existence of a ghost, plant the idea in their head—"

"By getting someone like Marcy to run all over town telling her ghost story."

"—then put them in the right state of mind and place, aim a couple colored lights at them, play some kind of spooky voice out of a hidden speaker—"

"Like this one?" Daphne said proudly. She showed me a cheap speaker she'd found hidden in a bush.

"Like that one."

"Okay, so we know *how* they did it . . . but how do we figure out who 'they' is?"

"I know where we start," I said, and told her what I'd heard from Milford Jones about the make and model of the car Marcy stole.

Daphne flinched, and then shook her head. It was the same expression of disbelief she'd worn when she thought Marcy was secretly dating Shaggy.

"What?" I prodded her. "Remember, if it's not impossible, it's possible."

Daphne rummaged through her bag and pulled out a small photo album. "My mom gave this to me—it's pictures of her from her first summer here. When she was only a little older than us, visiting Aunt Emma. That was the summer they both met men they ended up marrying." She flipped it open to the last page. "See?"

I saw, all right. On the left facing page, Daphne's mom and dad shared a bench in the town square, eating ice cream and gazing into each other's eyes like they were the only two people on the planet. On the opposite page, Emma and

Dr. Hunter stood hand in hand, gazing at each other with the same disgustingly romantic look. All of them were impossibly—or at least improbably—young.

But that wasn't what Daphne wanted me to see. It was the car Emma and her future husband were standing in front of: a vintage Mustang, cherry red, mint condition.

DAPHNE

VELMA WAS THE ONE who remembered that the Hunters kept their Honda on the curb even though their house had a garage. A garage that, supposedly, was so filled with a bunch of old junk there was no room left inside for a car.

But I was the one who had the inside line to Emma Hunter's secret history—who could ask my mother about the red Mustang. I was the one who got us the answer we were both dreading: "You bet that was Emma's Mustang. It's her baby—you've never seen her drive it because she wouldn't dare. She loves that car too much to risk it in the wild these days. Even then, she only took it out to get washed or serviced. I'm sure it's locked up tight."

That was teamwork, right? The two of us piecing together

the puzzle, hurtling toward a solution that both of us desperately hoped was wrong.

"I just can't believe it," Velma said. We were standing on the curb outside the Hunters' house, steeling ourselves to get some answers.

"See, I told you we had plenty in common. I can't believe it, either. Except . . ."

"Except I think it's true," she said.

And I thought she was right. I couldn't believe it and I didn't understand it, but nothing else made sense.

Now we just had to decide what to do about it. We'd considered calling the cops, or trying to tell our parents . . . but what would we tell them? We had no hard motive, no evidence, no clue where the missing girls were, no idea how some musty old librarian and his Martha Stewart–worthy wife would have ended up mixed up in something like this. Who would listen to us until we had something irrefutable to offer? There were no reinforcements to call in. There was just the two of us. Standing outside the house of the world's least likely criminals. An absentminded professor and my favorite (and only) godmother.

We had to be wrong. And there was only one way to find out.

We'd come here to try to get into the garage—the professor was at work, and Emma was having afternoon tea with my mother. Perfect timing for a little breaking and entering.

We didn't even have to break anything—the garage door was unlocked. Easy enough to pull it up and step right inside.

Still, I hesitated. It was one thing to suspect them of a crime. It was another thing to commit one ourselves. And I was pretty sure that breaking into their garage when they weren't home counted as some kind of crime. What if we were wrong? What if we got caught?

Velma looked at me like she knew exactly what I was thinking. "Second thoughts?"

"And third and fourth and fifth, but . . ."

". . . but all of them end with, 'let's do it anyway'?"

"Exactly," I admitted.

She nodded. "So let's do it anyway."

We went inside.

The garage was indeed packed with junk, cardboard boxes and stacks of books and rusting gardening equipment. But not so much junk that there wasn't also room for a bright red Mustang. It was in perfect condition.

"Is it possible it's a coincidence?" I said. "This car doesn't look like it's been in an accident—"

"Look at this bumper," Velma said. "It's got to be brand-new—look how much shinier and cleaner it is than the rest of the trimmings. And look at the paint job here, on the hood—look close. It's not the exact same shade of red as the rest of the car."

"I'm having it repainted as soon as the correct paint color

comes in," Emma's voice said behind us. We whirled around. *Total panic.*

Emma, on the other hand, seemed perfectly calm. Was she innocent after all? Or was she just so certain of not getting caught that she wasn't worried about us suspecting her? "May I ask what you girls are doing sneaking around my garage?"

Velma opened her mouth, shut it again, so that wasn't going to be much help. It was on me to fix this. However certain of herself Emma might have been, she wasn't an idiot. It had to have occurred to her that we were here for a reason. Maybe that we were onto her. I needed a distraction. *Fast.* So I did the only thing I could think to do.

I started to cry.

* * *

I wept. I wailed. I hugged Emma and held on like I was drowning in the Pacific and she was an Emma-shaped lifesaver. Trust me: There's nothing like a good meltdown to get you whatever you want.

"Honey, honey, it's okay," she murmured, and I kept fake blubbering like I didn't even hear her. "What is it, sweetheart? What's wrong?"

"I—I—oh—I—" That was key, too. You had to make them believe you were too upset to even explain it. Especially if you were trying to get someone to usher you into her living room, sit you down on the couch, and offer to make you a calming pot of tea.

"Y-y-y-y-es, p-p-p-p-lease, t-t-t-t-ea," I said, in the shudderiest voice I could manage. Anything to draw out the distraction and keep her busy while Velma took advantage of the situation and poked her nose everywhere it wasn't supposed to go.

"I'm going to go find, uh, a bathroom," Velma said. Fortunately, we were on the same page about her snooping around. Unfortunately, she was still as bad a liar as ever. I hoped Emma would think that she was just clumsily trying to give us some time alone.

There was no reason for Emma to suspect that we were conning her, and that while I was weeping into the upholstery and reminding good old Aunt Emma that she'd told me I could always come to her if something went wrong, Velma was ransacking the house for something that would explain what they'd been up to, and why. *Just go fast*, I willed Velma, because of course there was one good reason for Emma to suspect us: if she was actually guilty.

"I just feel like my mother loves her new family more than she loves me," I whimpered. The key to a good lie is to wrap it in a kernel of truth.

"Oh, Daphne, I know for a fact that's not true." She hugged me tight, and I wished all over again for us to be dead wrong, for Aunt Emma to be nothing more than the loving godmother I'd always thought she was. Because if her hug was also just a lie wrapped in a kernel of truth, it meant all this time I'd been even more alone than I thought. It meant even the people you most trusted could betray you.

"It's lucky I was here this afternoon," Emma said. "I was supposed to have tea with your mother, but I had a bit of an unexpected errand to run, so I had to cancel."

"Yeah." I sniffed loudly. "Lucky." *Let's hope.*

"In fact . . ." She checked her watch. "I'm sorry to rush you out, but I really should get going—I just need to grab something from the office and—"

"Dr. Hunter lets you into his OFFICE?" I practically shouted, hoping Velma would hear. "Wow, he seems like he'd be so finicky."

"Well, I'm not going in there to break anything, dear," Emma said laughing. "I just need to bring him something at work."

As she crossed toward the office, Velma popped back into the living room. When Emma wasn't looking, she gave me a thumbs-up. *Yes.*

"Wow, I feel so much better now, Emma!" I called. "Thanks for the words of wisdom and all, but we should get going!"

"Wait, I'll walk you out—"

But before she could, we were out the door.

We ran to the car, and quick as I could, I put it in gear, pulled out from the curb, and drove down the street, where hopefully Emma wouldn't notice it when she left the house.

I was careful to stay in range so we'd still be able to see her when she did . . . in case we needed to follow her.

As soon as I'd braked, I turned to look at Velma. "Can I just say, you're a genius?" she said, goggling at me. "Not to mention a very impressive actress."

"Please just tell me you found something? Or didn't find something—I don't even know what to root for."

"I found something. And . . . I took it." She laid out the evidence for me on the dashboard: Yellow flowers and a plant mister, from Emma's greenhouse. Printouts of emails between Dr. Hunter and a company called FunTime Inc., indicating that he was getting a *lot* of money for his services and that he was promising FunTime immediate results on the "tricky zoning issue."

"You hacked his computer?" I asked, not sure whether to be shocked or awed.

She shook her head. "At the library, Dr. Hunter always prints out his emails and makes me file them—I had a feeling he probably did the same thing at home. So? Now what?"

Before I could hatch a plan, Emma came bustling out of the house, carrying a gigantic picnic basket. She loaded the basket in the trunk and got into the Honda.

I gave Velma my most sharkish smile. This one, at least, was easy. "Now, we follow her."

I tried to keep one or two cars between us at all times, and as far as I could tell, she didn't spot us. But of course, there was no way to know for sure—and I had to admit, my car wasn't exactly inconspicuous. A silver Mercedes was the kind of car everyone spotted, and stared at, and admired, and remembered—which was the whole point of driving one. Except, of course, when you were tailing someone who might or might not be a kidnapper.

Emma was driving west, toward the coast, and sure enough, she pulled into the parking lot by the surfers' cove—and the tide pools. The professor was already there waiting for her.

Velma and I pulled the car in as close as we could without being seen, but the beach was deserted at that time of day, so that meant staying pretty far away. Still, we had a view of them venturing into the sea caves. Twenty minutes later, they came out again—no picnic basket—and drove away.

We stayed. For one very good reason.

"That's got to be where they're hiding them. Marcy and the Hex Girls," I said. The cave network went on for miles—there were caves that no one had ever mapped, darkness beyond fathoming. Where better to hide a few girls you needed everyone to believe were gone forever? Where better for Velma and me to get lost forever ourselves?

"Daphne . . . maybe this is too big for us," Velma said, and I could hear the conflict in her voice, the battle she was waging between wanting to help and wanting to run home, hide under the bed, let the grown-ups solve everything.

Or maybe I was just projecting.

We called the tip line that the cops had set up for information about the Hex Girls. (Anonymously, since I was pretty sure the cops probably had our names written down, filed under "hang up immediately.") The guy who answered sounded a little like Manny, the one we'd met in the station with Shaggy. He also sounded bored out of his mind.

"The sea caves?" he said. "And why are you so sure?"

"Because we followed the kidnappers straight there!"

"Oh, there's kidnappers now?" he said, voice dripping with derision.

We went back and forth with him, trying to persuade him of our theory, but pretty quickly, he interrupted. "Look, kids, this line is for serious tips only. Or at least it's supposed to be. We've got no manpower left to investigate your claim right now, and you know why? Because we're getting calls from all over town from meddling kids trying to 'help.'"

"We're not meddling kids!" I snapped.

"You may not be kids, I don't know, but you're definitely meddling. Point is, someone will come out there to take a look, eventually, but I wouldn't hold your breath. You want my advice?"

"No."

"Leave the detective work to the grown-ups." Dial tone.

I stared at the phone, incredulous—and enraged.

Velma shook her head. "Like I always say, most adults—"

"Yeah, yeah, can't wrap their puny, insecure brains around the idea that they might be wrong and a *teenager* might be right. The horror!"

Once again, we were on our own. And we knew what we had to do. But I very much didn't want to do it. I could tell Velma felt the same way. Still, what was the other option? Try and fail to persuade someone to take us seriously, over and over again? Let the girls rot away in the dark?

I knew Marcy was in there. I could feel it. "We have to go in," I told Velma.

"You're right. But first I think we have to make one more call . . ."

VELMA

WE STOOD AT THE mouth of the cave, preparing ourselves to venture into darkness. "We can do our part," I said. "You sure he can do his?"

Shaggy tugged at his dog's leash, and Scooby barked eagerly. "Like, if Marcy's really in that cave, Scoob is the one to find her."

"She's in there," Daphne said. "I know it."

We still only had circumstantial evidence, but I knew it, too. And at least with Scooby on our side to lead the way in—and hopefully out—we had a chance.

"You really think she's okay?" Shaggy asked.

I waited for Daphne to answer, but she didn't say anything. I could see why. Her eyes were blurry with fear. She didn't want to think about all the unknowns, and I didn't blame her. "This all seems to be a money-making scheme," I told Shaggy. "I don't think they'd actually hurt anyone."

But how did I know? I never would have expected Dr. Hunter to do *anything* like this, so it seemed pretty obvious I didn't know him at all.

That was the thing I hadn't realized about being a detective—you realized how many people were just wearing a mask, pretending to be someone they weren't. Hiding the monster underneath.

Today, we would rip off the masks. Somehow.

Shaggy promised he'd left word for his mother, but she was out investigating other tips, and no one knew how quickly she'd be back in radio contact. We couldn't wait—even if I'd wanted to, I knew Daphne would refuse. And I wasn't letting her go in there alone.

"Okay, Scoob." Shaggy waved a sweater under the dog's nose—Daphne had found it in her trunk; it belonged to Marcy. She and Shaggy confirmed—it still smelled like her. "Find Marcy! Go!"

Scooby barked, strained at the leash, and charged into the darkness. We followed.

It was darker than I knew darkness could be. We used our phones to light the way, but it didn't help much—we could only see a few feet ahead of us, and "see" was a bit of an overstatement.

Scooby padded forward confidently, like he knew where

he was going, and I tried not to worry that he was following the smell of fish or some other tasty snack that would lead us to a watery dead end.

"Oof!" I stumbled and slammed into the ground, face-first. Everything stung.

"V! You okay?" Daphne was by my side in an instant.

I let her help me up, slowly, and tested that my limbs were all in working order. But unfortunately . . .

"My phone cracked," I said. One less light to lead our way. "And so did my glasses."

Without them, I was basically blind. Which shouldn't have mattered so much in the dark. But it did. The world was fuzzy—and about a hundred times more terrifying.

"You want to go back?" Daphne whispered. I shook my head, then realized she probably couldn't see and said no. Out loud.

"But I can't really see anything."

"Take my hand," Daphne said. "Trust me."

We walked slower after that, inching along in the dark for what felt like forever, and then, suddenly, Scooby barked. It echoed through the caves.

"Whoa, like, Scoob, where are you gooooing—" Shaggy's voice faded, like he was getting farther away.

"Shaggy?" I said, panicky.

"Shaggy, slow down!" Daphne called.

"I can't, like, Scoob is on the scent, and I gotta . . ."

I could hear the dog running, I could hear Shaggy's footsteps pounding, and then . . . nothing. Just the sound of my breathing. And Daphne's.

"Daphne?" I whispered, in a very small voice. I couldn't see *anything*. If she ran off to follow Shaggy and Scooby—

She squeezed my hand. "I'm not leaving your side."

We inched through the dark. I kept one hand on the slimy cave wall. It was reassuring, knowing there was something solid, other than just the black. It was not reassuring, however, that the cave wall kept getting wetter, the deeper we ventured in. What if some of these caves were flooded? What if we were walking straight into the sea?

Then Daphne stopped abruptly.

"What is it?" I whispered. It was horrible not to be able to see where we were going.

"The cave branches off here," Daphne said. "And I don't know which way they went."

I shuddered. If we chose wrong, we might never find Shaggy and Scooby. And we might never find our way out again . . .

"Shaggy!" Daphne shouted, her voice echoing.

I winced at the noise. It felt like we should be as silent and sneaky as possible. But I told myself that wasn't rational. The Hunters weren't waiting for us in the dark. And neither was a ghost or any kind of sea monster. The darkness was just darkness. Not scary.

Okay, *very* scary. But not dangerous.

I hoped.

"Shaggy!" I called out, as loudly as I dared. "Scooby!"

It felt good to hear the sound of my own voice. I shouted louder. "Shaggy! Scooby!"

That's when we heard it. Not an echo. A bark.

"This way!" Daphne said, and pulled me along faster than before.

"Daphne!" Shaggy shouted back. "Hurry!"

"Daphne!" That wasn't Shaggy's voice.

It was a girl's voice. One I recognized.

"Marcy?" Daphne didn't let go of my hand, but she tugged me forward. We followed the sound of the voices around one more turn, and there they were, close enough that even I could see: Shaggy, Scooby . . . and the missing girls. All four of them. Terrified . . . and bedraggled . . . but alive. Okay.

Daphne flew into Marcy's arms and the two of them clung to each other.

I'd thought I'd be jealous. I'd worried that if we ever actually found Marcy, there would be a tiny part of me that was sorry, that knew Daphne would probably ditch me for her all over again. But I was wrong. Not even a tiny part of me was sorry. I was just so relieved for Marcy that she was okay. And so relieved for Daphne that she'd found her friend.

"How did they get you here?" I asked the Hex Girls.

"They must have dosed us with something during the concert," Thorn said, confirming my suspicions. "We all started hallucinating, seeing, like, ghosts or something. And then, I don't know. I think maybe I passed out?"

"We all passed out," Dusk said. "And when we woke up, we were tied up here, in the dark."

"With the infamous Vanished Girl," Luna said. "Who it turned out wasn't so vanished after all. She's the one who told us it was the old guy and his wife. Though I still don't get what they wanted with *us*."

"I keep telling you; it's not about us," Marcy said, sounding almost like herself—by which I mean, *mean*. She was rubbing her wrists—Daphne had just finished untying the last of her bonds, while Shaggy and I helped Thorn, Luna, and Dusk. "It's some kind of stupid real-estate scam. They're just trying to scare the crap out of Crystal Cove so they can get what they want."

"Well, they managed to scare the crap out of me," Luna said. "Can we discuss how we're going to get out of here?"

"Scoob will find our way out just like he found our way in," Shaggy said. "Won't you, Scoob?"

Scooby barked happily, and Marcy let go of Daphne just long enough to give him a hug. The dog licked her face, slobbering all over her tears. "I love you, too, you dumb dog," she said, laughing.

But suddenly, Scooby whimpered. It was a noise that sounded like danger. We all fell silent, listening intently.

"What is it, Scoob?" Shaggy whispered. Then, to us, "Uh, guys, I think he hears something."

In the ensuing silence, we all heard it. A car engine. It was faint, but distinctly echoing through the caves.

"They just left to get more water," Thorn whispered. "They said they were coming back."

"There's more of us than there are of them," Daphne said. "I'm not scared."

"What if they have, like, a weapon?" Shaggy asked.

"They've got whatever they dosed us with," Dusk said.

"She's right," Marcy said. "They spray us with one whiff of that stuff, and we don't stand a chance."

"What if . . ." I had told myself I was just bringing it for emergencies, but this seemed to qualify. I pulled out the plant mister, which I'd filled with water and freshly crushed flowers. "What if we dose them first?"

Daphne nodded. She looked impressed with my forward thinking. "We spray them and run for it!" she said.

"And then what?" Marcy countered.

"Then we go to the cops!" I said.

"You don't understand." Marcy sounded desperate. "No one will believe us. They're smart—they have plans and backup plans for everything, and they'll be able to talk their way out of it."

"They kept telling us they'd let us out once they got their money," Dusk said. "That they'd *rescue* us. It was like they weren't even afraid of getting caught."

"I bet they're planning to make it sound like whatever you accuse them of, you just hallucinated it," Daphne said bitterly. "Who would believe a bunch of teenagers over two reputable adults?"

It sounded diabolical—but it also sounded like it might work.

Marcy nodded. "The only way they're ever going down for what they did is if they randomly march into the police station and confess."

"Huh. Then I guess that's what we're going to have to make them do," Daphne said. She was standing close enough that I could almost make out her face. I squinted, certain without my glasses I was seeing it wrong.

"Are you smiling?" I asked.

"You bet."

"Not to ask a stupid question, but . . . *why*?"

"Because I think I have a plan."

DAPHNE

IT WAS DARKER THAN dark. Quieter than quiet. All in all, your basic nightmare. I pressed myself against damp stone, breathed shallowly, tried to hold myself perfectly still, waited for danger to arrive. I kept expecting my eyes to adjust to the darkness, that shadowy outlines of the other girls would reveal themselves, but shadows require light, and we had none. Every second lasted a year.

I'd started to wonder whether it was a false alarm when we heard it. Footsteps, picking their way across graveled earth. Murmuring voices, familiar, getting louder.

"How much longer can this go on?" Dr. Hunter's words floated toward us, too close.

"It'll take as long as it takes." That was his wife, my godmother, the woman I'd called Aunt Emma since I was old enough to talk, and who I'd so often compared favorably to my mother, wishing my mother could be soft and warm like her. But she was speaking in an alien voice, a voice like steel. "Screw this up for us and you'll be sorry."

My blood went cold. She sounded like a stranger. An inhuman stranger who didn't care who got hurt. Especially if it was someone—or a bunch of teenage someones—standing in her way.

I tried to be ready. Any minute now.

"Why is it so dark up there?" Emma said. "There should be a light." The footsteps quickened. I caught the shine of a flashlight beam.

Velma squeezed my hand: the signal.

Now.

Now or never, I thought, and reminded myself that these people had kidnapped my best friend, and three other girls, and terrified the town, and there was no one but us to stop them.

As they stepped through the mouth of the cave, I raised the spray bottle, took aim, and hit them both in the face with a hallucinogenic mist.

Dr. Hunter sputtered. Emma screamed and staggered backward. Her flashlight dropped to the ground and rolled away. Perfect.

Now, I thought, hoping everyone remembered the plan—not to mention hoping Velma had been right about how the spray would take effect.

As one, the Hex Girls begin to howl. Shaggy and I aimed our phones' flashlights at the roof of the cave, skimming the beams across the stone.

"The cave is on fire!" Emma screamed.

"What is it?" the professor whimpered, in a frightened, childlike voice that sounded entirely unlike his own. "What is it what is it what is it what is it?"

The howls rose and echoed, Emma cried something about getting out, and as they both began to back away, the howls cut off, and a deep, booming voice filled the cave.

WAIT.

I shuddered. It sounded like something deep and primal—nurturing an ancient rage—emanating from the stone. Who knew Shaggy had it in him?

STAY WHERE YOU AAAAAAAARE.

They stayed. That was when I relaxed, just an inch, because if they were obeying a mysterious voice coming from the darkness—no matter how old and angry it sounded—that meant the flower mist must have worked, and they were just suggestible enough to fall for their own tricks.

YOU HAVE DONE VERY BAD THINGS.

"Who are you?" Emma whispered. "Wh-what is this?"

WEEEE ARE THE SPIRITS OF CRYSTAL COVE.

The Hex girls improvised an *ooooooh*. I approved.

YOU HAVE SINNED IN OUR NAME. NOW YOU MUST BE PUNISHED.

"No!" the professor cried. "Let us go!"

He sounded scared out of his mind—but it was like his brain couldn't process the obvious next step, which was simply turning around and making a run for it. He'd been ordered to stay, so he stayed.

Was it possible this would actually work?

YOU SHALL GO NOWHERE UNTIL YOU, LIKE, UH—

There was a pause, and then I heard Velma whisper the next line in his ear.

ATONE. YES. THAT'S IT. ATONE. YOU WILL CONFESS YOUR SINS, OR YOU SHALL BE SEALED IN THIS CAVE FOREVER, ALONGSIDE YOUR FOREFATHERS.

I hit RECORD on my phone and crossed my fingers.

"It was her idea!" the professor shrieked.

"Of course it was my idea!" Emma shouted at him. "Everything's always my idea! If it was up to you, we'd probably be living in caves, surrounded by your pathetic books. I deserve better."

"Oh great, now we're starting on what you deserve?"

"I deserve millions. I deserve an empire. You want to go after someone, spirits, how about you go after Elizabeth Blake? She may have stolen my idea, but she stole your story. Got rich off us both. That stupid, spoiled daughter of hers gets to live in luxury while I'm stuck with . . . this? No."

It was like a punch in the stomach. Velma squeezed my hand again. No signal this time, just a message that I understood: *We can get through this.* And when we did, I would think about those words, think about the bitterness and rage in her voice when she said my mother's name. When she said the words *stupid. Spoiled.* Later, I would think about how this woman had pretended to love my mother for all those years, secretly nurturing that kind of hate. How she had pretended to love me. How I had been so desperate for love that I'd fallen for it.

Not now.

SO WHAT DID YOU DO? SPELL IT OUT FOR THE SPIRITS.

This time, Scooby-Doo was the one who howled. Hopefully, they'd think it was a hellhound preparing to drag them into the darkness.

"We drugged people into thinking they saw ghosts, okay?" Emma said.

AND?

"We kidnapped some girls, fine! But it was all harmless! We just wanted what we were owed. And Crystal Cove deserves all the money it can get, too. This town is pathetic, settling for less than it could get, all to honor what? A bunch of founding fathers too clueless not to die?"

"No offense, spirits," the professor said. "But she's right. Preserving local character is a fool's mission. Change is inevitable. The future is upon us. There's no reason not to pursue whatever the land is worth."

WE ARE THE REEEEEASON.

"We're sorry!" they both yelped.

That's when Velma and I aimed the flashlights at our faces. I wanted them to know who'd stopped them—to know that betrayal had consequences.

Emma squinted in the sudden light. "What are *you* doing here?"

"We're not here," Velma said. "We're manifestations of the spirit world."

"Spoiled, stupid manifestations," I spat out, seething.

Velma shot me a look. "We're here to deliver you to justice," she said.

"Justice?" The professor's voice cracked. "Nooooo!" He turned on his heel and fled into the dark.

"Don't leave me alone with it!" Emma screamed, and raced after him.

"Scooby, like, after them!" Shaggy shouted, and then all of us—boy, dog, no-longer-missing girls, me, and Velma, half-blind but with her hand firmly wrapped around mine like she trusted me to lead her—took off, chasing shadows through the darkness.

We ran through the damp, ran through the cold, ran around corners. Velma tripped, stumbled, nearly fell, but I caught her weight and pulled her along, heart thumping, lungs tight, darkness closing around us.

Then finally, finally, the pitch-black faded to gray, and I

caught a whiff of fresh sea air. We blasted through the mouth of the cave and into the light.

Just in time to see the professor and Aunt Emma fly straight into the waiting arms of the police.

"Arrest us! Put us in jail where we'll be safe!" the professor begged them.

"Shut up!" Emma snapped, but it was too late. The cops were doing just as they'd been asked.

I sucked in a deep breath, and as all the tension fled my body at once, I realized a part of me had been dead certain we'd be trapped in that dark forever. Judging from the look on Velma's face, she'd been thinking the same thing.

"How did the cops know to be here?" I asked, looking around for Shaggy's mother. I figured his message had finally gotten through. But the only familiar face I spotted through the crowd of uniforms was—

"Milford Jones? What are you doing here?"

"Ask your pushy friend," he said, nodding at Velma. "She's the one who tipped me off."

I turned to Velma. "*You?* Called *him*?"

She blushed, and then shrugged. "You're the one who said we should take help wherever we could find it. I figured he could help."

"Unlike some people"—Milford shot a disdainful glance at the cops—"I can tell when a story's too good not to be true. So while you were dealing with Shaggy, I called in the cavalry. Not everyone respects me. But *everyone* listens to me."

"Thank you for everything, Mr. Jones," Velma said, though I could tell it was killing her to owe him anything, especially gratitude.

"You can thank me with that exclusive you promised," Milford Jones said. "How about you start by explaining to me why it is some old professor and his wife would turn themselves into kidnappers and poltergeist-fakers? Because that's a story even I couldn't concoct."

"You don't need us to explain that to you," I said, showing him the recording on my phone. His eyes lit up like he'd won the lottery. "Because the kidnappers and poltergeists will explain it themselves."

I pressed PLAY. Then I handed Velma the phone. Let her give the interview and tell him how we'd saved the day.

As for me, I was feeling the sudden urge to give Marcy another hug, and this time maybe I'd never let go.

DAPHNE AND VELMA

DAPHNE

The cops were the ones who found it. After they searched the scene of the crime—and all the other crimes—they searched the scene of the criminals. Rumor has it they tore apart the Hunters' whole house, looking for evidence against them. Which seemed ever so slightly unnecessary to me, given the whole "caught red-handed" thing, not to mention the whole "confession captured on audio thanks to my extremely genius plan" thing—not that I was expecting a reward or an official commendation or something. (For the record, I got neither.) But I guess the police wanted to be thorough. And maybe, like everyone else in town, they were just a little angry they'd nearly gotten bamboozled into believing in ghosts, or at least been freaked out enough to think, in the private dark of night, that it might be possible.

Anyway.

They searched Emma's greenhouse and took her flowers into evidence as dangerous weapons. They searched every one of the professor's boring archives—and that's where they found something not so very boring. Well, technically, it was still pretty boring, just a stack of legal documents that were so old and dusty and filled with out-of-date jargon that no one knew what they meant. Fortunately, there happened to be a lawyer in town who specialized in real estate and was feeling guilty enough that he was willing to work pro bono.

Which is how my stepfather ended up summoning me to his office and greeting me with a smile wider than the Grand Canyon. He handed me a photocopy of one of the documents. "The original has to stay in the file," he said, "and there'll be an official notification, but I had a feeling you might want to be the first to pass along the good news."

"What good news?" I said. I said it nicely. My stepfather and I weren't exactly BFFs or anything, but we were getting along. It turned out once I stopped hating him on general principle, there was a lot to like. We had the same taste in late-night TV, and I had to admit, he made a mean pancake.

I also had to admit it wasn't the worst feeling in the world to sit around the breakfast table with my mother, my stepfather, and my two half-sisters, passing the maple syrup, pouring the orange juice, feeling almost like a family.

"That's a deed to the land the Haunted Village sits on," he said. "A legally enforceable deed."

"Okay . . . and?"

"And take a look at whose name is on it."

VELMA

"Dinkley!" My father stabbed at the photocopied deed with his index finger, joyous. "What did I tell you! It's Dinkley land through and through!"

"Sí, mi amor. You told us so." My mother patted him on the back, and then caught my eye. We were both trying not to laugh. It was challenging—partly because once the shock wore off, my father had started his mildly hilarious *told you so* routine, and forty-eight hours later, he was still going strong.

Mostly, though, I wanted to laugh out of sheer joy. I hadn't seen my father this energized, this *alive*, in years. And yes, I knew it wasn't a magic fix. But even if it wasn't a permanent change, even if it wasn't permanent happiness, it was still evidence that change was possible. It was proof that the old him, the healthy, happy him, was still there inside him, and wanted to come out.

Before Daphne's stepfather found the deed, proving our family owned the land we used to live on—proving that my father's family legend had been right all along—had seemed impossible. Like it had seemed impossible that Dr. Hunter, who I'd foolishly thought was my friend, had been keeping the deed from me all along—or that it would turn out my real friend, my best friend, for a second time around, would be Daphne Blake. That Daphne would be the person who finally did exactly the thing she promised me she'd do when we were ten years old and she found me on her back porch, sobbing that our family was going to have to move away—that when Daphne showed me what her stepfather had found, I would throw my arms around her without hesitation, without worrying whether she'd hug me back. That she would hug me back.

It had seemed impossible that my mother would get her job back, but wouldn't even need it anymore—much less that my mother and father would suddenly have the power to decide whether the Haunted Village stayed in business at all, or whether it would pack itself up and move off our land for good.

It had seemed impossible that my family would ever have choices again, that we would ever have the chance to get back some of the things we'd lost.

If all that was possible, then maybe anything was.

DAPHNE

It took a lot of whining and pleading, but I got Marcy to let me throw her a going-away party at my house. A very, very small going-away party, given that there was a very, very small number of people Marcy actually liked.

We invited the Hex Girls, with whom she'd bonded during their time in the cave, at least once she got them to stop singing the fear away at the top of their lungs. Shaggy, of course, who Marcy had finally agreed to hang out with in public—but had still not agreed to kiss. At least according to what she'd told me, and she'd also told me we were done keeping secrets from each other, so I believed her.

Velma came, too. Not that she and Marcy had a single nice thing to say to each other—but maybe once you save someone's life, and/or get saved by them, mutual hatred is harder to sustain. I got the feeling they might do their best, though. Or at least they would have, if Marcy was actually staying in town.

Even at her going-away party, I couldn't believe she was actually . . . going away.

Her parents were there, too. They didn't exactly fit on the short list of Marcy's favorite people—or, at least, she never would have admitted it if they did—but Marcy was leaving, and they were the ones taking her as soon as the party was over. So it seemed simpler to invite them. That's what she told me, at least. But I had a feeling, from the look on her face every time her mother asked if she was okay or her father smoothed her hair, that she had reasons of her own to want them around. She'd be seeing a lot of them, soon.

It turned out your daughter getting blackmailed and then kidnapped made for a pretty big final straw—after all this time, Marcy's parents had come home for her. And now they were taking her home with them, across the country, and then who knows where. They weren't the type to stay in one place for long. Marcy wouldn't say so, but I knew she was happy about it. And that made me just a tiny bit less sad to see her go.

I still wanted the party to last forever, because once it was over, Marcy and I would be, too. You can't stop time, though. One by one, people started to leave. I watched, from a perch on the stairs, as Marcy said goodbye. She gave Shaggy an extra-tight hug, and I saw her whisper something in his ear. He nodded, then kissed her on the forehead, very gently, and turned away. I still didn't understand what was between them—but it was clear, even from where I was sitting, that it was a lot.

"Okay, Blake, your turn," Marcy finally said, summoning me. I walked toward her, feeling a little like I was walking toward my own execution. This didn't have to be the end of anything, I reminded myself. People could stay friends, even if they lived in different cities.

Though the best evidence I had of that was my mother and Aunt Emma, which . . . wasn't exactly comforting. I shook it out of my head and focused on the present. *Marcy.* One last time.

"Promise you won't forget me?" she said as we hugged goodbye.

"Swear."

"And you won't replace me with Velma Dinkley, of all people?"

"No one could replace you," I assured her, and that was the total truth. Velma wasn't going to replace Marcy any more than Marcy had replaced Velma all those years ago. I loved them both. And somehow, even after all we'd been through, after everything that had been said and done, both of them loved me back.

It was weird, how even on the day one of your two best friends in the world was leaving you behind, maybe forever, you could still feel lucky. You could still feel loved.

Marcy squeezed tight, and then slipped something into my hand. "For after I'm gone," she said.

And then, all too soon, she was.

Afterward, Velma found me on the back porch, trying not to cry. "You okay?" she said, sitting down beside me.

I nodded. "You don't have to stay."

"I owe you one," she said, and I wondered if she was remembering the night I'd found her out here, crying about her family losing their house. I'd promised her we would figure out a way to fix it. All these years later, we finally had. Together. That made me feel a tiny bit less sad, too.

"Marcy gave me something just before she left," I told

Velma. "A note. A secret, I guess. But I don't think she'd mind if I told you."

I unfolded the paper Marcy had slipped me and handed it to Velma. She pushed up her glasses—the new ones were always sliding down her nose—and squinted at the small print.

Shaggy needs your help.

"That's rather mysterious," Velma said.

"Seriously." The best I could figure was that Marcy wasn't the only one who'd confessed a secret in that friendship. And Shaggy wasn't the only one who'd sworn a vow of secrecy. "So what do you think we should do?"

Velma put an arm around my shoulders and held on tight, just like she used to. I could hear my mom in the kitchen, singing as she put away the leftovers, just like she used to. And for a moment, past collapsed into present—as if *everything* was the way it used to be.

I shook the thought away. I couldn't go backward. And for the first time in years, I didn't want to. I wanted to see what would come next.

Velma studied the note like it was in code. Maybe it was. "It's a mystery, right?" she said. I nodded. "Then I say we do what we do best. We solve it."